# Why?

**Why** did heiress Brenda Benton ask beautiful young Helen Manning to be her roommate?

**Why,** after Brenda's mysterious death, was Helen suddenly courted by Vic Wales, once a great concert pianist, now a bitter young man with an injured hand and a three million dollar legacy?

**Why** did Chuck Fedder, the obscenely fat, spectacularly successful public relations man, give Helen a glamorous job with his organization?

**And why,** as Helen fell under the spell of the famous public figure, John Markham, did danger close in around her like a strangling hand in the dark. . . ?

# Scared to Death

# Scared to DEATH

## Rae Foley

A DELL BOOK

**For Beth Gillen**

Published by
DELL PUBLISHING CO., INC.
750 Third Avenue
New York, New York 10017

Copyright © 1966 by Rae Foley
All rights reserved. No part of this
book may be reproduced in any form without
permission in writing from Dodd, Mead &
Company, Inc.
Dell ® TM 681510, Dell Publishing Co., Inc.
Reprinted by arrangement with
Dodd, Mead & Company, Inc.
New York, New York

Printed in Canada

First Dell printing—April 1971

*The characters, places, incidents, and situations in this book are imaginary and have no relation to any person, place, or actual happening.*

# ONE

As THOUGH he had some forewarning, Bill Benton began to talk the night before he died.

Tom Keith, as he had done every night since he joined them, went to bed drunk. Watching the change in the good-looking, reckless face from day to day, Victor Wales was grimly aware that his friend was headed either toward chronic alcoholism or d.t.s. He was beginning to wonder how one coped with delirium in the heart of the Rocky Mountains, seventy-five miles from help.

As though answering his unspoken thoughts, Bill said abruptly, "Of course, we could always knock him out."

"He's taking care of that himself," Vic grunted.

"You can't altogether blame him."

It was basic in Bill's character, as it had been in his twin sister's, to blame no one. They were both protectors of the weak. There were always circumstances beyond control, unknown factors that explained or mitigated. Not that Bill was a sentimentalist, Vic thought; he was simply hell-bent on whitewashing the human race. The acknowledgment of a flaw was like a crack in the fabric of his universe, one that in time might cause the whole thing to break up.

Vic had watched in sardonic silence the mental gyrations by which his friend maintained not so much an emotional stance as an emotional wobble. For Bill the process of explaining human behavior was a dogged effort to explain away anything that interfered with his theories.

"If I'd been married to Mary and had lost her," Bill went on, "I'd be half out of my head too."

All three of them had been in love with Mary who, from the beginning, had never been interested in anyone but Tom Keith, who was, Vic conceded, a good-looking devil, one of the black Irish with fine features, deep blue eyes, and startlingly dark brows like slashes across his forehead. Tom with his wild gaiety, his irresistible smile, his unbridled spirits. He was, Vic thought, like an unbroken horse. In an earlier age he would have been another musketeer, edging D'Artagnan out of the limelight, just as, in a still earlier age, Bill Benton would have belonged to the Round Table; that is, if one could imagine a cross between a knight in armor and an eighteenth-century Methodist theologian. Bill was a moral crusader tempered by romanticism.

In that he was the counterpart of his twin sister, Brenda. One of the half-dozen things that had made the camping trip in the Rockies an outpost of hell had been the necessity to maintain a careful silence about Brenda. Several times since his recent arrival, when he had been working hard to tie one on, Tom had attempted to talk about her, but Bill might have been deaf. Knowing him so well, Vic was sure that Bill thought of little else, particularly since Brenda's recent and shattering death by drowning.

The telegram announcing her death had been sent to Sheridan where they went once a week for supplies. That time Vic made the trip. In fact, he was gone five days. As he was not a man accustomed exclusively to masculine society, Bill made no comment on the length of time he had been away.

Vic collected the telegram along with letters for Bill and a number of overdue bills for himself that had accumulated at the post office. Bill retired to the tent with his mail and the telegram. When at last he appeared his voice was almost expressionless.

"Brenda is dead. She was drowned on Sunday at Mary's house on the Connecticut shore. On our birthday. They weren't sure when word would reach me, so they've gone ahead with the services and all that."

He wheeled and went away, walking fast. It was

dark by the time he got back and sat down to eat the meal that Vic had waiting for him.

Early the next morning he announced his decision to go to Sheridan. He seemed to be in a tearing hurry.

"You go ahead," Vic said. "I'll break camp and come along later."

"What for? There's nothing to go back to now, is there? I have a couple of things that need attention and then I'll rejoin you."

When he returned it was, surprisingly enough, with Tom Keith. Tom had turned up in Sheridan and not so much asked as demanded to join the other two men.

At first Vic had been inclined to welcome him. At any time Tom was a good companion; he would help pull Bill out of the curious mental state into which he was sinking. But by the second day it was apparent that Tom, instead of filling his usual role of cheerer-upper-in-chief, was in need of comfort himself. The unbelievable had happened. Mary, the wife to whom he had been passionately devoted for six years, had left him.

By day the three men—rather idiotically, Vic began to think—went grimly on with their self-imposed activities: hunting, fishing, scrambling over the mountains. By night they retired into their separate, morose silences.

That night, as usual, Tom had staggered into the tent and fallen on his cot in a drunken sleep. Vic and Bill sat staring at the fire whose brightness dimmed the stars. For a moment Bill's face was illuminated as he struck a big kitchen match to light his pipe. Whether it was the play of light and shadow or some change that had occurred during the past three weeks, Vic was shocked by the gauntness of his cheeks, the hollows under his eyes, the look of despair. Like a condemned man, he thought.

Unexpectedly Bill laughed. "I was just thinking, Vic, we're three men in the same boat. Running away. Every mother's son of us. You because you can't play any more piano with that crippled hand, Tom because Mary has destroyed their wonderful marriage, and I because Brenda is dead." As though deliberately hurting himself, he added, "And dishonored."

There wasn't, Vic reflected, any reply to that. He groped for cigarettes, hauled one out of the package awkwardly because of his maimed hand, snapped his lighter.

"I've got to talk to you, Vic. You'll have to stop running away, as of now."

"I've never thought uplift was quite the right field for you, Bill. Suppose we all go to hell in our own way. Anyhow, this set out to be a vacation, not an escape hatch. Let's keep it that way."

"Vacation! Like hell it did. I had to get away from the news hounds sniffing on my trail. Tom had to get out of New York where he was afraid he would run into Mary. *Forever and Yesterday* will be going into rehearsal soon. And if this wake has seemed like a vacation to you, you've been successful in concealing the fact. You're as grim as the Reaper himself."

There was no point, Vic thought, in probing old wounds. The intelligent thing was to prevent yourself brooding over them. In time, with luck, they stopped hurting, and a little scar tissue never did anyone any harm. He flicked his cigarette into the fire and started to get up.

Bill seemed taken aback by that sudden movement. "Wait, Vic! Don't go to bed yet. I've got to talk to you."

"You look seedy to me. We've all been overdoing lately. Why don't you turn in for a night's rest? We can talk tomorrow."

"Not with Tom helling around all day until he gets drunk. That's the trouble with the Irish. If they're not cock of the walk, they're in the lower depths. Anyhow, tomorrow and tomorrow and tomorrow— it's never wise to count on them. In fact, I'm not counting on them. I'm counting on you."

Vic subsided with a grunt. For a man who liked women as much as he did he usually found male companionship less demanding. Men, as a rule, did not pour out their inmost thoughts and yearnings in a spate of words. Being emotionally self-sufficient himself, he had little sympathy with the compulsion for wordy self-exploration.

Down the mountainside a waterfall spilled noisily, a rush of sound. Around him in the dark the great mountains soared. As a rule he took comfort in their vastness, their permanence, their bleak beauty. Tonight they pressed in on him like a threat and he was annoyed with himself for feeling it. Beethoven might have cried out his exultant, "Holy, holy, holy!" in this place, but Vic had a smothered feeling that the mountains were bending over him, prepared to crush.

He was exasperated to realize that he was losing the sanctuary that the mountains had meant to him, that had led him to seek them: the peace, the stillness, the remoteness from emotional problems; a peace to which he was determined to cling. He wished that Bill would let the past alone, but he knew that tonight, come hell and high water, he was going to talk about Brenda, drag out the whole baffling, unsavory business, and probably try futilely to understand what had driven his twin sister to behave as she had done. For his own peace he must absolve her.

"I meant to do it myself," Bill said abruptly, "but I counted on having plenty of time. Thing is—you know the last trip I made to Sheridan? Well, I had a —quite an enlightening interview with a guy there and found some mail from David Case. You know David, don't you?"

"No."

"Nice guy. Quiet and unassuming, but with a gift for friendship. There doesn't seem to be a field of human activity in which he hasn't friends. I used to think he and Brenda would marry, but something went sour. David believes it was because she was in love with someone else. Of course, David doesn't have much—uh—romantic appeal. You know the sort of thing women like." Bill grinned. "You ought to with your batting average."

"Look," Vic said with an edge on his voice, "I do not, repeat not, collect scalps."

"Okay. Okay. Maintain absolute calm. Anyhow, to get back to David Case. His old man was the Benton lawyer. David took over after his father died. He handles Brenda's legal business and mine. I had to make a new will, of course. The old one is no good now. Brenda and I left everything to each other." Like pressing on a sore tooth, Vic thought uneasily. "Thing is, I've made you residuary legatee."

"For God's sake, Bill!"

"Hold on. Before you blow your stack, let me explain. In the first place, the only living relations I know of are my mother's cousin, Nora Ellis, and her daughter Bessie, who are strictly poison. Anyhow, Mother left them each a nice legacy when she died, which takes care of that. In the second place, I'm not giving you anything for free. It's payment for services. And if what I suspect is right, you'll earn every penny."

"Considering that you are six years younger than I, this is academic, isn't it?"

Bill made a queer little sound that was not quite a laugh. "That remains to be seen. Anyhow, I've left it to you because you're just the kind of fool who will go ahead—what's the line?—'Though hell should bar the way'—to earn your money." He drew a long breath. "Vic, thing is, I want you to learn the truth about Brenda. No—wait! I knew that gal. She was protecting someone. Find out whom she was protecting and then, by God, you'll find out who murdered her!"

Vic jerked as though he had touched a live wire. "Bill!"

For the first time Bill laughed with his old gaiety and there was genuine amusement in his voice. "I'm not off my rocker. But I've been thinking—an unusual exercise for me, as you'd be the first to point out—and I've reread that last letter of Brenda's. David found it on her desk and mailed it to me after she died. It was the queerest thing, Vic, getting a letter from her when she was gone. By the way, it's in my wallet and I don't want anyone but you to see it. That clear?"

"Okay. Keep your shirt on, Bill. I just—"

"Wait." There was something feverish in the younger man's manner and Vic wondered whether he was really ill, whether his haggard appearance meant more than the strain and grief that had followed Brenda's notorious dragging through the public press and her fatal accident.

"I'm waiting."

As usual, his relaxed manner steadied his friend. "You'll see Brenda's last letter for yourself, and there are some others in my suitcase. I'll tell you where to find the rest of the stuff."

"Did she explain why she refused to testify before the Congressional Committee?"

"No, she didn't. The worst of it is, Vic, that I'm sure she would have explained if I had been there. We had always been close—most twins are, I suppose—but I had to raise a stink when she took that job with Fedder. He and his wife weren't Brenda's sort. Don't snort! I'm not being snobbish. It wasn't simply their vulgarity, not even mainly that. It was a kind of spiritual shoddiness that, well—you knew Brenda."

Yes, Vic had known Brenda; ardent, romantic, and, most of all, impressionable.

"Anyhow," Bill said, "we had a knockdown and drag-out fight over it. She said she was old enough to lead her own life. So then, when the case broke and Brenda was in it up to her ears, she refused to discuss it with me. When she was called up before the committee and just sat there, mum, I couldn't believe it. All she was ever willing to tell me was, 'I can't help it, Bill.' Then, with the news hounds baying on my trail, I cut and ran to join you out here.

"Well, that's all water over the dam now. We patched things up, of course, and she's been writing, but . . ." His voice trailed off. "And now they've silenced her for good."

"I suppose," Vic said, managing to keep his voice even and relaxed, "you know what you are talking about."

"How much of the Markham case did you follow?"

"Considering that we don't see any newspapers and you smashed the transistor radio the day you got here, I know very little about it."

"At least you know Brenda took a job with Chuck Fedder. She wanted something amusing to do and she was fascinated by Fedder because he was so unlike anyone she had ever known."

"She fell for Fedder?"

"Good Lord, no! I think we can both guess at the identity of the man she fell for, Vic. But let that go. Fedder is a big, gross fellow with a lot of bounce and bonhomie, loud-spoken, jovial, with his fingers in a lot of pies. Public relations. He goes in for crazy stunts, the kind of thing that brings the newsmen running. Remember the fake fire with all the red smoke that brought out three companies of fire equipment when he was doing publicity for the book *Fire Alarm?* He nearly got jugged for that one. In fact, no one knows how he keeps out of the toils of the law. Brenda said he just shouts with laughter and makes people feel like fools if they can't take the joke in the right spirit."

Vic grunted. "That guy is spoiling for a kick in the teeth. A practical joker is the lowest form of so-called human life."

"Then when a Midwest politician was running for governor he pulled that business of the robbery in the guy's house, with our hero protecting his family and battling the burglars singlehanded. Later the opposition tracked them down and proved they were a bunch of unemployed actors, but by that time the politician had won the election and called it just good clean fun."

"And for a man like Fedder your sister let herself be pilloried?"

"It wasn't for Fedder," Bill said. "I'm sure of that if of nothing else. It couldn't have been Fedder. He would never have had so much influence over her. No, I think she fell in love with Markham and took it right on the chin to protect him. She wouldn't lie, but she could keep still. Damn his soul to eternal hellfire."

Vic got up to pour bourbon, add water, and hand one glass to Bill, taking a long pull at the second. Bill went on slowly as though he were arranging what he had to say.

Brenda had been amused when she first started working; she had loved the erratic hours, the feverish excitement, even the absurdity of Fedder's wilder publicity stunts. It had been like watching a three-ring circus with bands playing and fireworks exploding and bright-colored balloons bobbing around in the air.

The scandal had broken without warning. One day John Markham had been an impeccable figure, a government trouble shooter, a presidential adviser, an incorruptible man who stood above the crowd. The next day there were rumors that he had peddled influence, that he was responsible for the awarding of a contract for army clothing, and that he had received a hundred thousand dollars from Horace Ralston, president of the company that had obtained the contract. The intermediary with whom he was said to have worked was Chuck Fedder.

The toppling of a man like Markham from his high eminence had shaken the whole country. If that monolithic figure could be dishonest, where was honesty to be found? There were "lost leader" editorials and cartoons with the legend, "Just for a handful of silver." But worst of all was the general lapsing of confidence in the integrity of the government itself.

Vic remembered clearly his own sense of shock and outrage and a feeling that was almost personal grief and shame for the blasted reputation. Though he was congenitally disinclined to believe in the myth of "the essential man," he had come close to thinking Markham indispensable.

Markham had denied any knowledge of the affair. He had fought valiantly to clear himself, but it had been like fighting fog. The purchasing committee had denied that any influence whatever had been applied, which might mean something and might not. They had, after all, their own skirts to clear. No reliable evidence appeared; there had been more smoke than fire. A Congressional Committee investigated and in the end brought the hearings to a halt without coming to any conclusion. But Markham resigned, went back into private life, discredited and dishonored.

Chuck Fedder, who had figured as the *deus ex machina,* denied indignantly having any knowledge of the affair. His faithful assistant, Brenda Benton, refused to testify. Day after day she had appeared before the committee, standing stubbornly mute.

The affair dwindled from page-one headlines to the back pages and then disappeared. Public attention shifted to trouble in Vietnam, in Africa, in India. Then Brenda was drowned.

"Well," Bill said, "to get back to her letters. Most of them aren't much help. There's a little here and there about the Fedders and David Case and especially about Helen Manning, some girl who moved into the apartment with her after I came out here.

"The last letter was in the apartment. She hadn't had a chance to mail it, but David found it and sent it on. She said, 'I've learned something about Helen that changes everything. And by the way, I've left a record in the usual place. Just in case.' And across the bottom of the page she scrawled, 'They've tried to kill me, Bill. I'm scared to death. I've been horribly wrong. Please come back.'

"That's all, except for David's wire saying she had drowned accidentally. Well, she didn't, Vic. That gal could swim like a dolphin. Someone killed her to keep her quiet. I want you to find out who it was."

Inside the tent Tom's cot creaked as he turned over. Bill lowered his voice. "There's one thing more. Brenda wrote some time ago saying that Mary had been going around a lot with John Markham. That's why I didn't want to say anything about this to Tom. Having her leave him like that was tough enough without knowing it was for Markham. I'm worried about him. He's the kind to bump himself off in a moment of despair."

"Not Tom."

"You're wrong," Bill said quietly. "If ever a good guy was destroyed by a woman, Tom's the one."

"I'd go a long way out on a limb for Tom," Vic said, "but I won't be talked into seeing Mary as a man-destroyer. It simply can't be done. There isn't a trace of meanness or malice in the woman."

"You're still in love with her, aren't you?"

"Everyone loves Mary," Vic answered lightly.

Something in his tone made Bill demand, "Have you believed a single word I've been saying?"

"I don't think you've been lying to me, if that's what you mean."

"You know what I mean." Bill stretched wearily and yawned. "Oh well, you're stuck with it now, like it or not. Let's get some sleep. I'm dead on my feet." Vic heard him laugh as though at some private joke. "Tomorrow there are a few things I'll have to explain to you, and then we can forget about it until we return home."

"Tomorrow," Vic said, "we're heading for Sheridan and the first plane out."

"Then you do believe me!"

"I believe you're a sick man, Bill." Vic lunged forward, grabbed the younger man's wrist, looked at the automatic that had dropped to the ground. "What the hell is that in aid of?"

"I have a pretty grim idea."

"I have a couple of ideas too." Vic slid the automatic into his own pocket, dragged Bill to his feet, looked at the haggard young face. He steered him toward the tent, eased him onto his cot.

Bill opened his eyes and grinned. "Over to you," he muttered, and fell asleep.

Across the tent Tom turned on his back and began to snore.

Moving noiselessly, Vic went outside to throw water on the fire, to see the stars grow brighter as the coals faded, to watch the night close in around him. He turned the automatic over and over, his hand tightening around the metal grip.

## TWO

THE HUMMING increased in volume and Vic said irritably, "Stick to the cello, Tony. If you're going to warble your way through the Twelve Variations, I'm quitting. Let Casals sing. Let Glenn Gould sing. But I'm not playing with a damned tenor. Now let's take it again from the beginning and try to keep your mouth shut."

Once more they began the statement of the theme. The humming stopped. There was a kind of rustling and someone cleared his throat. Fingers found Vic's pulse. He opened his eyes and looked into the strange face that was bending over him. A young, rather unformed face. Saw the white jacket.

His heart jolted and he saw that the intern was aware of it. This was it. From now on he had to be alert, on his guard. He took one swift look around the hospital room, saw the heavy-set nurse staring at him with a queer look of speculation on her face, felt the twinge in his leg as he moved. It was a relief when the fingers left his wrist. He could control his expression; his pulse betrayed him.

"Is he—" the nurse began.

"Oh yes, he's conscious," the intern said. Something in his voice made Vic feel that it would be wiser to keep his eyes open. You can't play possum with a doctor.

"Where is this?"

"Hospital. Sheridan, Wyoming."

"How did I get here?"

"That's quite a saga." The young doctor grinned. "First, Forest Rangers; second, a truck; finally, an ambulance."

"What's wrong with my leg?" Vic asked fretfully.

"You had a bullet in it," the intern said.

For a moment Vic panicked. "How—bad?"

"Hit the shinbone. We've done a graft. You'll walk again."

Vic didn't like the intern's tone. He didn't like it at all. He didn't like the look of avid curiosity on the nurse's face. One thing was clear: these cold-blooded angels of mercy didn't care whether he ever walked again. They didn't think it really mattered. Something was wrong. Something had gone horribly wrong.

He didn't need to prod his memory. Every incident of that morning—how long ago?—was crystal-clear. Clear, that is, up to the time when he had fainted.

The humming sounded again and he realized that it was some electrical equipment in another room.

"Don't you remember anything?" the doctor asked, still with that sardonic expression. "Who shot you?"

"Bill," Vic said slowly. "It must have been Bill. He was sick. Out of his head. He went—berserk, I guess. What happened to him?"

"He's dead," the intern said. "Dead as mutton." No attempt to soften the blow. Almost as though he wanted to see how Vic would react.

"The poor devil. The poor devil."

14 SCARED TO DEATH

The intern glanced at his watch. "Okay," he said to the nurse, "the patient is able to talk now." He went out of the room without looking back.

The man who came in was not in uniform, but police was stamped on every line of his body, on his bearing, on his watchful eyes. On the whole, the interview went better than Vic had expected. Bill had been acting rather strangely for several days. The sudden death of his twin sister had been a tremendous emotional shock. That morning Tom Keith had been the first to get up. He had gone out to gather wood for a fire, a job which they took in rotation. Vic was pulling on his pants when the bullet struck him in the leg. He had fallen on his cot and then—curtains.

"Then how," the detective asked smoothly, "did you get across the tent to Benton? You were lying practically on top of him with one hand clutching his shirt when you were found."

Vic looked at him in bewilderment. "I was?"

"The Forest Rangers were only about a hundred yards away when they heard the two shots. They shouted and came on the run. Met your friend Keith tearing toward the tent. When they got inside they found Benton shot through the heart, and you were hanging on to him. You had passed out with a bullet in your leg."

Vic shook his head. "I don't remember a thing after I was shot."

The detective shrugged. It was, he declared, a very queer setup. The automatic was lying beside Benton's hand; it was, incidentally, his own weapon. Had there been a quarrel? Good lord, no. All three men had known each other since they were kids. Never any trouble after they passed the schoolboy scrapping stage.

"That's what Keith says."

"Where is Tom?"

"He stayed until he knew you were going to be all right and then he had to get back to New York. You won't be out of here for a matter of weeks. That leg is going to need therapy."

Vic let his eyelids droop wearily, but the detective was a slow man to take a hint. He settled himself more comfortably beside the bed where he had a good view of Vic's face.

"Benton," he said thoughtfully. "Brenda Benton was his sister, wasn't she? The girl who was involved in the Markham affair?"

Vic nodded without opening his eyes.

"What did Benton think of that performance?"

"He didn't understand it, but he believed in his sister. He thought she was protecting someone."

"Well, that was clear enough. Protecting herself."

Vic's eyes were wide-open now. The detective wasn't missing anything there was to read on his face.

A young nurse came in, smiling, with a box of magnificent red roses. "Someone must like you," she called gaily. She handed Vic a small envelope and began to arrange the flowers in a tall vase. Vic held the little envelope, turning it in his hand, puzzled. Who would send him flowers? He knew nobody in Sheridan. For some reason he was reluctant to open the envelope in the detective's presence. The latter sat with his eyes on it, expectant, waiting.

At last Vic was forced to draw out the card. He recognized the big untidy scrawl at once. The message was brief, only five words: "Take care of yourself. Love." It was signed Mary.

He lay staring at it in startled speculation. Without ceremony the detective reached for it. "Mary?"

"Mary Smith. Tom Keith's wife."

"The musical-comedy star? That Mary Smith?"

"That Mary Smith."

"Another old friend?" The question was casual.

"We all—Tom and Bill and I—have been friends since we were youngsters, as I told you. As Tom's wife, Mary naturally fitted in."

"Naturally."

Vic began to feel uneasy. Fortunately the hard-faced nurse appeared with a tray and said, "Doctor says you're to eat just as much as you can manage. Otherwise we'll have to go back on glucose." She wound up the bed, guided the bent glass tube to his lips, and he began to sip clear hot soup.

This was obviously going to be a slow process, so the detective, with a casual, "Be seeing you," went out. After he had finished lunch, for which he had a surprisingly robust appetite, the bed was wound down again, the curtains drawn against the brilliant sunlight, and Vic slept.

He was awakened when the door opened and a middle-aged man slipped into the room, as though trying to escape notice. Reporter, Vic thought immediately. Careful.

"You Victor Wales?"

"Yes."

"How did Benton happen to shoot you?"

At least there was no soft approach, no cautious groping for position. The disillusioned eyes watched him as he talked.

"So all you remember is that Benton suddenly went berserk and you got a bullet in your shin when a shot went wild."

"That's about it."

"Old friends, weren't you?"

"As you say."

"This Keith a friend of yours too?"

"Yes."

"Husband of our glamorous Mary," the reporter commented, and Vic stopped himself just in time. Don't let him make you lose your temper, he warned himself. "Lucky for Keith that he was out of range when Benton started shooting. I've done a bit of checking. There were rumors that before our glamorous Mary picked Keith, you and Benton were fairly assiduous in your attentions."

Well, there it was, Vic thought. Mary was being placed in the center of the stage.

"Fairly assiduous in your attentions. That I should live to see the day when a reporter talked like that!"

"It's this here higher education. What set Benton off? The death of his twin sister?"

"Apparently."

"That was a queer business. She evidently got herself tangled, but tangled, man, with quite a setup."

"I wouldn't know."

The reporter laughed. "He wouldn't know. Look, brother, let's not pretend that Brenda Benton was any sheltered innocent. She was a rich gal who wanted to do something for kicks. Looks like she got more than she expected."

"I wouldn't know." Vic moved restively as his leg began to throb. "Look, I'm willing to be co-operative, but I have a smashed shinbone and I'd like to rest."

"I see your point, but look at mine. We don't often get celebrities here, so celebrities are still news. William Benton, millionaire; Brenda Benton, mixed up in the Markham case; Tom Keith, married to America's most popular musical-comedy star; Victor Wales, one of the big concert pianists."

"Not any more."

"Yeah." The eyes seemed to be all over Vic's face. "Your right hand was broken, wasn't it? Ended your career."

Vic grunted.

"How did it happen?"

"A fight," Vic said levelly.

The eyes were thirsty for information. "For a guy like you it must have been important if you'd risk your hands."

"I was drunk."

"*In vino veritas*. A kind of violent type for a musician, aren't you?"

"What type are musicians?" Vic countered.

"I wouldn't know." The reporter quoted Vic with a chuckle. "You're sure Benton shot you and himself?"

"Who else? I was unconscious."

"Yeah."

"Why the hell," Vic snarled, "would I kill Bill and shoot myself? That's what you are trying to get at, isn't it?"

"Yeah, the violent type," the reporter commented softly. "You're in a spot, brother. There was a news flash from New York an hour ago. Benton made a new will just before he died, leaving everything he had to you. So there you are: you had a motive for killing Benton, but Benton had no motive for killing himself."

And that was when Vic got his only break that day. A doctor whom he had not seen before came into the room, a tired, middle-aged man with a kindly mouth and x-ray eyes.

"I am Dr. Medley. Did your friend Benton mention me?"

Vic shook his head.

"He came to Sheridan to consult me. I ran through a series of tests. He had leukemia—only a short time to live. Didn't he tell you?"

*Dead on my feet.* Bill had laughed at that.

Vic stared at the doctor, lips white. "He knew?"

"Oh yes. Took it remarkably well, I thought. At least at the time. But there must have been a delayed shock, more than he could handle. Undoubtedly that accounts for his crack-up and suicide."

II

They had gathered in David Case's office for the reading of the will. The Ellises, mother and daughter, as the only remaining blood relations, had constituted themselves chief mourners, and they had dressed for the part in deep black.

Nora Ellis was a large angular woman of sixty with faded blue eyes, yellowed white hair, and a mouth that looked as though she were tasting something unpleasant. Her daughter, Bessie, was in her middle thirties, already beginning to fade without ever having blossomed. At this moment her eyes were filled with tears—Bessie cried as easily as she breathed—and her childish mouth quivered. Nora had kept Bessie childish until she was in her twenties —"Trying not to rub the bloom off the peach"— and Bessie had retained her infantile qualities as a kind of defense against a disconcertingly adult world.

Bessie now sat with her ankles neatly crossed, her eyes downcast, as though she were in church, black-gloved hands clasped on her lap. She sniffed continuously and maddeningly. Her mother put a hand on hers.

"Now, dear," she said consolingly, "you must really stop crying. I know how you feel about darling Bill, but you must be brave."

Bessie blew her nose and summoned up the brave smile of a twelve-year-old child. "I just keep thinking of the dear boy and how he used to come to our house for Sunday dinner. You know how much at home he always felt. Just like having a brother of my own."

"I know. You were devoted to him and he was devoted to you. It's perfectly natural. After all, we were his only family, the ones who loved him the most."

Having established this point, Nora Ellis looked challengingly at the two other people whom young David Case had summoned to his office. She and Bessie were Bill's only relations. If Tom and Mary Keith got any substantial inheritance, she would know the reason why.

In spite of her alarm lest she be defrauded, Nora could not keep her fascinated eyes off the couple. As she had observed happily before, Mary Smith lost most of her glamour and nearly all her beauty when she was not on the stage. The afternoon sun revealed the skin with its pores enlarged by grease paint. Without the big warm smile, the vitality and joy that crossed the footlights like a flame, she was simply a rather plain young woman, and today a haggard one. Absolutely ravaged, Nora told herself in delight.

Tom Keith looked tired and drawn. Well, Nora thought in satisfaction, it served him right. Poor little Bessie had been infatuated by his good looks and his charm. How the child had suffered. How she had cried. But Tom had never even been aware of her. He had never noticed her adoration. No, he had to run after an actress, and much good it had done him. Everyone knew now that Mary Smith had left him for another man.

Tom was trying hard to catch his wife's eyes, but after the first startled moment when he had entered the room, she had paid no attention to him. She merely said, her voice so flat and low it was barely discernible, "Hello, Tom," and took a seat as far away as she could. Tom pulled his chair close to hers, but she did not once turn to meet his imploring eyes.

David Case came in and sat down at his desk. He was slight and fair and looked younger than his thirty-five years, although his hair was already thinning. He turned from face to face. It occurred to them that he was a very angry young man.

He cleared his throat. "I suggested that you come here to listen to the reading of William Benton's last will and testament, because each of you is mentioned in it and I thought there might be—questions."

Tom's eyes turned from his wife's averted face to that of the lawyer with a look of sheer astonishment. Never before had he heard a lawyer hint that a client's will might—should?—be challenged.

Mary Smith sat motionless with the poise that her stage training had given her, wide eyes fixed on David Case. Tom wondered whether she saw the lawyer, whether she saw anything beyond her own somber thoughts.

"This," Case went on, "is, as I said, Bill's last will and testament. It was drawn up just a few days before he died by a local man in Sheridan, Wyoming. The lawyer sent me a covering letter from Bill. Of course, after Brenda's death it was necessary to draw a new will as Bill had made her chief legatee. Then, too, he had inherited everything of hers, so the estate has become a fairly impressive one. I suppose his haste in making this new will without waiting to consult with me was due to having learned, as he wrote me, that he was dying of leukemia."

Tom caught his breath in a gasp that was like pain. "Why didn't he tell us?"

Case shrugged. "I wish to God I knew." Then he began to discuss the terms of the will. There were bequests for medical research, for an old retired cook, for a former gardener who was now pensioned but still, at his own request, carried on as caretaker for the Connecticut house.

"To Thomas Keith," Case read aloud, "the sum of twenty-five thousand dollars.

"To Mary Smith Keith the sum of twenty-five thousand dollars.

"To my mother's cousin, Nora Ellis, the sum of one thousand dollars.

"To her daughter, Bessie Ellis, the sum of one thousand dollars."

"Why, the—" Bessie began sharply. Her mother's hand tightened on her arm in caution, and she fell silent.

"The rest of my estate, whether in real estate, stocks and bonds, in whatever form, including my car, my co-operative apartment in New York City, and my house in Connecticut, together with their furnishings, I bequeath to my friend Victor Wales."

"Oh, I'm so glad!" Mary exclaimed, her famous husky voice startling in the quiet office. "So glad. Dear Vic. He can't play any more, but this will compensate to some extent."

Looking at the lawyer, aware that he was hoping to have some protest made, some attempt to break the will, Tom let out a shout of delighted laughter. "Good for Bill! And good for Vic. Now he can get out of debt and start all over again."

Then Bessie, disregarding her mother's restraining hand, wailed, "It should be ours! It should all be ours. We're the only ones related to him. His own blood. We ought to fight that will."

Nora Ellis pushed back her chair as she stood up. "Look here, Mr. Case, this is outrageous, and what's more, I think you know it. Bill always was flighty and easily managed. Impressionable, like Brenda. They were always the same. There was undue influence in making that will. Don't tell me Victor Wales didn't work on that poor sick boy as soon as he knew his condition. Why, according to the stories in the press, Bill must have been out of his mind when he died. Out of his mind. That will can't stand."

For the first time Mary turned to Tom. "Was he, Tom? Was Bill out of his mind?"

For a long moment the two looked at each other. "He was certainly beside himself toward the last," Tom said. "But I don't believe he was crazy when he drew his will. I am sure he intended Vic to have his estate."

"Of course you'd back him," Nora snapped. "Old friends and all that. Anyhow, you probably think he'll see you get a cut for helping him out. But you can't fool me. Wales pulled a hard-luck story about his broken hand and Bill fell for it. He was always a pushover for a hard-luck story. Always stupid. Like Brenda. I'll fight it. The sentimental young fool!"

"Don't try," Tom advised her. "There is nothing sentimental about Victor Wales. He'd make a monkey of you. Isn't that true, Case?"

David Case, straightening papers on his desk, made no reply.

"But only a thousand dollars," Bessie choked.

"We were counting—we expected at least—why, how much is there, Mr. Case?"

"There will probably be somewhere in the neighborhood of three million after taxes, aside from the house and the apartment and the car, of course."

"Who is living in the Connecticut house now?" Nora demanded.

"No one," the lawyer said in surprise. "Ferguson, the caretaker, checks it every day, but he has his own apartment over the garage."

"Then Bessie and I are moving out there tomorrow. We'll see whether Victor Wales dares put Bill's own family out." She added in throbbing tones, "In the cold," a statement that lost something in drama as the New York temperature hovered in the high eighties.

Mary, pulling on her gloves, turned slowly. "Dares?"

Nora smiled. "It would be interesting to know just what happened out there at the camp when Bill died."

"What do you mean by that?" Tom demanded.

"Well, everyone takes it for granted that Bill shot Victor Wales and then killed himself." Nora added sweetly, "You didn't see the actual shooting, so how do you know it happened that way?"

## THREE

SUMMER DRAGGED on, an endless succession of days of pain and therapy, of graduating from bed to wheel chair to crutches and, finally, in September, to the triumphant use of a single cane.

Little by little the reporters lost interest in Victor Wales; even the police stopped dropping by to see him. The newspapers had no further references to the tragedy at the mountain camp. Bill Benton and his sister Brenda faded from the news, faded almost from memory.

*The New York Sunday Times* arrived at midweek and Vic scanned it in vain for indications that either death held any further public interest. Now and then there was mention of Mary Smith's new musical, which was in rehearsal. Now and then a fleeting paragraph appeared about John Markham, the former presidential adviser whose career had been destroyed by the rumor that he had accepted a bribe. He was said to be writing a book. He was quoted as conducting his own investigation in order to clear his name. He was seen dining with Mary Smith.

Now and then Vic received one of Mary's brief scrawls, Tom wrote in his telegraphic fashion, and David Case sent legal documents to be signed. It all seemed very remote.

Late in October, Vic, leaning on the new cane that he had carefully selected, limped off the plane at La Guardia Airport, a stewardess solicitously holding his arm, and was taken back to find himself facing cameramen, microphones, and a barrage of questions.

How did he feel about his inheritance? . . . What did he have to say about his accident? . . . What did he know about the strange silence of Brenda Benton at the Congressional hearing? . . . What did he think about John Markham's involvement? . . . Was it true that he would never again be able to perform as a concert pianist?

"No comment." Vic brushed them aside and climbed into a taxi, his luggage stacked on the front seat, the reporters still following him. He gave the address of David Case's office on Madison Avenue.

It was a glorious fall day, the air crisp and sparkling like San Francisco at its best, the sky a deep blue. Manhattan, when he arrived, seemed to blaze with light from the sun reflecting on glass-and-steel buildings. How beautiful the city was, he thought. He found himself whistling Vivaldi's Autumn theme from *The Four Seasons*.

The building was in the mid-fifties on Madison Avenue, a plush and glittering new structure, but David Case's suite was modest with a small reception room in which an obliging elevator man piled Vic's luggage.

The receptionist, a trim girl in her twenties, opened her eyes wide when she heard Vic's name. In a few minutes Case came out to meet him, looked him over as though, Vic thought in some amusement, he were checking for a shoulder holster, and shook hands gingerly. He didn't put out the welcome mat or greet Vic as though he were a valued client. Instead he treated him like a time bomb that might go off at any moment. Vic seated himself across the desk in Case's office and settled his leg as comfortably as he could.

"I think you'll find everything in order, Mr. Wales. I'm glad you came in so that we can go over matters in detail, unless you would prefer to leave that to your own lawyer."

Vic's eyebrows shot up. He lighted a cigarette, studying Case over the flame of the match. "I have no lawyer of my own," he said at last. "I rather expected to leave everything in your hands. Bill regarded you highly as a personal friend as well as his lawyer, and I know he was satisfied with the way you handled things for him. I'm no businessman myself and I'd prefer to leave it to you. If that's all right."

When the pause had dragged out uncomfortably he asked, "Any reason why you would rather not have me as a client?" He was amusedly aware of his unkindness, conscious that the lawyer was flustered and did not know how to control the situation.

"Oh no. No, of course. I just assumed you would prefer—that is—well, suppose we go over the main points so you'll know where you stand. The will has been probated and the estate settled. Both estates, Bill's and Brenda's. There was nothing particularly complicated, in spite of the size, so you can take over at any time."

Under Vic's ironic gaze the young lawyer became more embarrassed. "Oh, by the way"—he tossed a thick envelope across the table—"this came for you some weeks ago."

Vic glanced at the envelope, marked "Please Hold," turned it over to inspect the seal, pushed it back. "Keep it for me, will you? I had intended to consult you about it today, but perhaps that had better wait for another time. When I need it I'll let you know."

Case turned to fiddle with the combination of his safe and put the envelope in a cubbyhole. For the next hour the two men went over papers while Case explained investments, stocks, bonds, mortgages.

"It's a lot of money," Vic said at last soberly. "A lot of responsibility."

"I always thought Bill Benton was a singularly responsible person until—"

"Until he made that last will."

Case looked across the table to find Vic grinning at him. "By the way, have you made a will of your own?"

"Not yet."

"Who is your next of kin?"

"Not a living soul," Vic said cheerfully. "I'll let you know the main provisions in a few days."

"I hope you will. With an estate this size it would be terribly confusing if you died intestate."

"Then suppose you draw up a tentative will. Word it as you like, but everything to Mary Smith Keith."

This time Case was jolted out of any semblance of control. His jaw dropped. Then he swallowed and made a note. In an obvious attempt to regain the upper hand he said, "You will probably want to draw some money right away." His tone was impeccably polite and meant to be insulting.

"That's right."

"I'll introduce you at the bank so you can cash a check at once. And while we're about it . . ." Case fumbled in a drawer and pulled out a bunch of keys, each one tagged. "House, apartment, car. I'll have the car delivered to you today. Where will you be staying?"

Vic's eyebrows rose. "At the apartment, of course."

"You have a driving license?"

"Yes."

"That leg won't make it difficult for you to drive?"

"I don't think so. I hired a car in Wyoming and took a few short drives to get away from the hospital."

"You had a long siege of it." The idea did not seem to displease Case. He leaned forward, pale eyes intent behind the rimless glasses. "How in hell did it happen, Wales? I can't see Bill shooting anyone. He and Brenda were intrinsically gentle people. In fact, it's impossible to believe that he was capable of violence. And he would no more kill himself, regardless of what he had to face, than—"

"Than Brenda would."

"There was no question of Brenda committing suicide," Case said angrily.

"Were you there when she was drowned?"

"Can't we let her alone?"

"No."

"What are you trying to do, Wales?"

"Stir up the animals."

"What is that supposed to mean?"

"Self-protection. If I don't do it, someone else will. I'd prefer to be at the wheel myself than to be taken for a ride. I haven't much choice."

The lawyer scowled. "I'm not much good at riddles. As for Brenda, the poor girl went through hell. If you have any decency, man, let her rest."

"Let's assume that I have no decency. I want to know how Brenda died."

28  SCARED TO DEATH

"She died of drowning." As Vic waited, Case went on reluctantly, "It was her birthday, and Mary Smith gave a small party at her house on the Connecticut shore. Brenda went in swimming too soon after lunch, got cramps, and drowned."

*That gal could swim like a dolphin.*

"Getting information out of you is like pulling teeth."

Case was exasperated. "There isn't any information. I don't know what you are getting at."

"Who was there?"

"I was there. Mary Smith, naturally. The Ellises, mother and daughter. Not," he added by way of parenthesis, "that anyone wanted them, but Brenda was nice about things like that. After all, they were family. The Fedders were there, and Helen Manning, the girl who shared the apartment with her after Bill left."

"Who else?" After a considerable pause Vic repeated impatiently, "Who else?"

"Horace Ralston showed up."

"Ralston? The clothing manufacturer who got that government contract?" Vic's eyebrows nearly touched his hairline.

"He wasn't invited," Case said quickly. "He has a summer place not far from Mary's, and he just sort of dropped in. She couldn't very well throw him out."

"I don't see why not."

"If you're suggesting . . ."

"I'm not suggesting anything," Vic said, "but I never saw a social situation Mary couldn't handle. What about Tom?"

"They're separated. Didn't you know?"

"Yes."

"Tom came just for a few minutes to bring a magnum of champagne for Brenda and to drink a toast. But he didn't stay after—"

"Well?"

"After John Markham arrived."

"Markham. The somewhat bedraggled white knight."

"Markham," Case said angrily, "is a good guy who got a rotten deal."

"Then why didn't Brenda say so? She could have cleared him. Or could she? Is that why she kept still?"

"She didn't confide in me." The hurt was still in Case's voice.

"You saw a lot of her, didn't you, during the hearings?"

"No one saw a lot of her during the hearings except possibly Helen Manning. What's your interest in this?"

"What's your interest in Brenda?"

"I loved her," Case said, his face very young and curiously defenseless. "She was sweet and trusting and gullible. I loved her. I wanted to marry her. Once I think she would have. But this thing happened and she was tied up in knots by someone."

"Who?"

"I don't know." Case's tone changed the subject. He pushed back his chair. "Shall we go to the bank? You'll want your money without delay."

"My thirty pieces of silver, perhaps?" Vic said smoothly.

"What do you want done with this luggage?"

"Send it to the apartment, will you?"

"Why—sure. Look here, I'd better warn you that Helen Manning is still living there. And that reminds me, the Ellises are staying at the Connecticut house."

"At least," Vic commented in some amusement, "I won't be lonely."

II

Vic spent the afternoon looking through a viewer at the newspapers on film covering the Markham affair. He lingered over a picture of Brenda standing tense and stubborn before the committee. He had forgotten how much she resembled Bill, but Bill had been a good-looking man and Brenda rather a plain girl.

There was another picture at which he looked for a long time. John Markham had been snapped as he was coming off a tennis court, a slim, well-set-up man of forty with a good mouth and chin, laugh lines around his eyes. An attractive fellow. Only a fool would have hazarded a brilliant career and the prestige that went with it for the immediate benefit of a hundred thousand dollars. Markham did not look like a fool.

Brenda's fatal drowning accident had caused a rehash of the Markham affair. There were no details about her death beyond what Case had provided. Mary Smith, musical-comedy star, had entertained a few friends to celebrate Brenda Benton's birthday. Among them had been Chuck Fedder, the public-relations man involved in the Markham case, John Markham, and Horace Ralston. The juxtaposition of the three names was damning in itself. The implications were that Ralston had been Mary's invited guest, not that his presence there had been accidental, as Case had insisted. Mary Smith seemed to have got into very queer waters indeed.

Bill Benton's death had caused less stir in the New York press than Vic expected. Vic's own version had been used. Bill had gone berserk with grief over the death of his twin sister, had, while temporarily deranged, shot his friend Victor Wales, the concert pianist, and then killed himself.

When the news had broken about Vic inheriting the Benton money, the stories changed. They were cautious but filled with innuendo. Victor Wales's dazzling career as a pianist had ended tragically when his right hand had been crippled. He was known to have a hair-trigger temper. Since his accident he was said to be hard up. Though he had made a great deal of money, he lived extravagantly.

With the revelation of Bill's leukemia, which provided a motive for his suicide, the references to Vic dropped out of the papers.

It was late afternoon when he emerged into the street again, hailed a cab, and drove to the Beekman Place building where the Bentons had owned a co-operative apartment. He had not visited it in several years, so he was surprised when the doorman stepped forward smartly to open the door and greet him by name.

"Your luggage came this afternoon, Mr. Wales, and Mr. Case had your car delivered. It's in the garage now."

"Good." Vic went down a step into the dim lobby and stumbled, losing his balance. The doorman caught his arm, steadied him.

"Thanks. I'd forgotten about the step. It's some time since I've been here. How did you remember me?"

"Saw your picture in the afternoon paper." There was an odd expression on the doorman's face.

Vic merely grunted and started toward the elevators, leaning heavily on his stick, his leg throbbing from the jolt he had given it.

"Mr. Wales." The doorman hastened after him. "There's a lady waiting to see you."

"Vic, darling!" It was Mary's husky voice. She had been sitting in a deep chair far back in the lobby. Apparently she had been there some time, for the ash tray beside her was overflowing with cigarette butts and a cigarette still smoldered. She ran across the lobby, her hands outstretched, kissed him on both cheeks, and then stood back to study his face. "You look like hell," she told him simply.

He burst out laughing. "The same inimitable tact."

He wondered, as he did whenever he encountered her after a lapse of time, what it was that made her so special. Who else could have become America's most popular musical-comedy star with a name like Mary Smith? She wasn't beautiful, not even particularly good-looking when he stopped to analyze her features. It was the husky voice that could rise to a comic treble and could drop to thrilling notes as deep as those of an organ. It was the big mouth with its warm, radiant, infectious smile. It was, above all, her vitality that charged the air with electricity. Everyone, as he had told Bill, loved Mary Smith.

"How did you know I would be here, Mary?"

"I saw the afternoon paper. And I'm furious! The beasts! Anyhow, I wanted to get hold of you before some of your females tied you up. Come have tea with me tomorrow at five. Will you, darling?"

"I'd be delighted. But why not stay now and have a drink with me?"

"No," she said sharply. "I want to talk to you alone and that Manning girl is there. I telephoned before I came. Anyhow..."

"Anyhow?" He smiled down at her.

"I don't want to go back there," she said somberly. "The place is full of ghosts." She glanced at her watch. "I must run or I'll be late for rehearsal. This past week has been frantic and it will get worse. But you will come tomorrow? Promise?"

"Nothing could keep me away," he assured her.

Under the avid eyes of the doorman she stood on tiptoe to kiss his cheek lightly, and then she was gone. Vic stared after her, his lips shaping a noiseless whistle. It wasn't like Mary to go all out. Not at all like her.

## FOUR

THE APARTMENT was on the tenth floor and had a fine view of the East River. That was about all that Vic remembered of it as he had never taken a great deal of interest in his surroundings. What he recalled most clearly was the gruff sound of foghorns, the muted noises of traffic. Always sound.

And that, he told himself grimly, will be enough of that.

As he put the key in the lock he had a curious feeling of reluctance to enter this place. He had no right here. He was an intruder. Then he walked into the short narrow hallway that led to the big living room.

It all came back to him now, the windows opening on the river to the east, the baby grand piano before them—he would have that moved out—a breath-taking New York panorama to the south, towers lighted at night—he could not recall ever being there before during the day—a part of the view cut off by the soaring United Nations Building.

A kitchen led off the hallway and there were two small bedrooms, each with its own bath. One of the bedroom doors opened and the girl stood looking at him.

*I have learned something about Helen that changes everything.*

Brenda had never had a chance against this girl. The first impact staggered him and then alerted him to danger. For some reason it relieved him to realize that she was not his type. His preference, in his casual relationship with women, ran to lush blondes.

Helen Manning was not a blonde and there was nothing lush about her. She was tailored from the smooth black hair, parted in the middle and drawn back severely, to the gray suit with its crisp blouse and the oxfords on her feet. Efficient wasn't the right word. She gave the impression of a young woman who lived in constant preparedness for emergencies. With the exception of Princess Grace he could recall no woman who could afford the stark severity of her hair style. In her case it merely emphasized the flawless oval of her face.

"Mr. Wales?" Her voice was light and cool.

"I take it you are Miss Manning."

"Mr. Case telephoned me after he left you—at the bank." There was mockery in her tone. "Your luggage arrived a short time ago. It was brave of you to come here."

His brows shot up, but he was wise enough not to accept the challenge.

When she found he was not going to speak she added, "The place is full of ghosts."

"Curious you should say that. Mary Smith told me the same thing not five minutes ago."

"You've seen her—already?" The question was impulsive and she regretted it immediately.

"She was waiting down in the lobby to welcome me home."

"How—nice of her."

"Wasn't it?" The mockery was in his voice now.

For some reason she was at a loss. "I'll finish packing in a few minutes, and then you can have your apartment to yourself."

"There's no hurry. I hope I haven't inconvenienced you."

"Not at all. A friend of mine is letting me take her little house in the Village while she is abroad."

"You are fortunate to have such accommodating friends."

This time her eyes came swiftly to his face, startling him. Instead of being dark as he had expected they were a clear gray, as cool as glass. They met his, recognized their mutual hostility. The two smiled at each other, rather, Vic thought, like the raising of foils in a salute between two fencers.

The telephone rang and she started toward it, stopped to give him an inquiring look that said, "May I? Of course, it's your telephone now." She wasn't, he thought, eager to answer the telephone in his presence, but he eased himself into a chair and propped the cane beside him.

"Yes? . . . Oh yes, Julie . . . Yes, he just got here . . . Well, I don't know. Shall I ask him?"

She turned, her hand covering the mouthpiece. "That is Julie Fedder. She—Brenda worked for her husband. She saw by the evening paper that you had returned and she wants me to bring you to dinner tonight. She and Chuck were devoted to Brenda and they—well, they wanted to welcome you home." Her voice didn't give anything away.

"Why not? That's very kind of them."

She nodded, spoke briefly, and put down the telephone.

"They're on Central Park West. I'll give you the address. Seven-thirty." She turned toward her bedroom, turned back. "The evening paper is there if you'd care to look at it."

His picture was on page three. If it hadn't been for the headlines and the cane, he doubted whether he would have recognized it. As a rule he paid little attention to his appearance. His face in the mirror was so familiar that it barely registered when he shaved. Now he looked at it in dismay. He had lost a lot of weight, of course. But what caught his attention and made him feel that he was viewing a stranger was the hard-bitten expression. He looked older than his thirty years. His eyes were hard and defiant. His mouth, twisted with anger when he had confronted the cameras, would, he thought, have made a child run screaming.

Unexpectedly he recalled a review of one of his early concerts, which had amused as well as embarrassed him. "It is rare," the critic had written, "to find a man who combines monumental technique, superb musicianship, and the physical glamour of a great actor."

No one would find that now. He had destroyed more than his right hand and his musical career in the years since that review had been written.

## BENTON HEIR ARRIVES IN NEW YORK
### FIRST STOP THE BANK

He did not go beyond the headlines. He put down the paper, noticed that it was rattling, and gripped the arm of the chair to steady his hand.

Well, he thought, it's what I asked for, isn't it?

II

Helen Manning's bedroom was as starkly neat as her person. Considering her air of general efficiency, it was unlikely in the extreme that she had left anything behind. Still it was the logical place to start.

The wastebasket contained only a few crumpled pieces of Kleenex. The dresser drawers were empty except for the lining paper and smelled faintly of some light flower fragrance, which was odd to associate with the machinelike Manning. Three-in-One oil would be more like it.

Under the heavy satin cover the bed had been stripped. Nothing in the bolster. Nothing under the mattress.

The wall-to-wall carpeting, Vic decided after a careful examination, had not been disturbed. The small bathroom, smelling of spicy bath salts, was spotless. Nothing in the toilet tank. Nothing strapped under the washbowl.

His leg was beginning to throb from stretching and bending, but he felt a sense of urgency.

*Tomorrow and tomorrow and tomorrow—it's never wise to count on them.*

He examined the back of the dressing-table mirror, the backs of the pictures, tilted up the chaise longue and the dressing-table bench and the small slipper chair. He wasn't particularly disappointed. The only surprise would have been if the girl had proved to be careless.

*I've learned something about Helen.* For three months Vic had been speculating about her—a pointless activity, of course, until he could see her for himself. The picture he had built up was of a rather colorless girl, pleasant, well-bred, conventional and sentimental like Brenda, the kind of person with whom she would have been likely to share her apartment, the kind she would have found congenial.

Whatever he had expected, it bore no relationship to the girl he had found in the Benton apartment. She was beautiful, she was intelligent, she was hostile. And she was, in some fashion, involved in the Markham affair. Her association with the Fedders indicated that.

Looking through the desk drawers in the living room, not because he expected to find anything, but because it would be stupid to overlook the obvious, Vic thought about the Fedders. They hadn't let any grass grow under their feet. They read of his return in the evening paper and asked him to dinner that same night. There must, he reflected, be a number of people who wondered what Brenda had told her twin brother, what Bill in turn had confided to the man to whom he had left his entire estate.

He had anticipated a little time in which to get his footing before he had to walk a tightrope, but they weren't giving him time. The action had already started.

He could no longer ignore the insistent pain in his leg and he decided to have a drink before he gave it any more exercise. In the other bedroom his luggage had been neatly stacked, the large case on the luggage rack. He hoisted a smaller bag onto the bed and unlocked it, looking for a bottle of bourbon he had packed.

Then he began to laugh. He had taken pains with his packing, making sure that he memorized the position of each item, and it had paid off. Helen Manning had searched his luggage. This was beginning to take on all the aspects of farce.

He looked forward to seeing her that evening. Sooner or later he intended to take her apart to determine what made her tick. A pity that she wasn't his type. He always believed in combining pleasure with business when he could. And Manning wasn't pleasure.

He took the bottle of bourbon into the kitchen

and noticed that he was limping again. He got out ice and mixed a drink. He was carrying it back to the living room when the two-toned chimes sounded softly and he went to the door, the drink in his hand.

"Now that's what I call service." Tom Keith took the glass from him and drank deeply.

"Son of a gun." Vic went back to mix another for himself. Then he dropped down on the big couch and hauled up his leg with a grunt of relief.

Perched on the arm of a chair, grinning at him, Tom glanced at the leg.

"What made him do it, Vic? When I heard those shots . . ." Tom shook his head helplessly. "And when the Rangers and I came in and found the two of you, we couldn't tell at first—" He broke off, his hand shaking so that the liquid spilled over the edge of the glass, but his eyes steady, intent.

Vic shrugged. "Who knows?"

"No point in speculating," Tom said heavily. "Of course, when you think of the leukemia—poor devil, why didn't he tell us instead of trying to take it by himself?—and Brenda dying like that . . . Well, I suppose we'll just have to forget it. Go on from here." He grinned. "That's easier for me than for you because you've still got that bad leg to remind you. How is it?"

"Not too bad. It bothers me right now because I've been giving it too much of a workout. They haven't cushioned the New York pavements yet."

"You've had a busy day, it seems."

Vic laughed. "If you read the evening paper, and everyone seems to have read the evening paper, you can probably recite my whole itinerary."

"What are they trying to do to you?" Tom spoke with unexpected savagery. "Put you in the pillory?"

"Just fun and games."

"There's enough nasty suggestion in that story to justify a suit for libel."

Leaning back on the down pillows, Vic sipped his

drink and studied his friend. For all the surface gaiety, Tom seemed ravaged, the rakish good looks blurred. "What have you been doing with yourself?" Besides getting stewed to the eyebrows. Vic didn't put that into words.

Tom shrugged. "Looking for a job."

"But I thought—"

"I was Mary's press agent. Remember? It would be a bit awkward for both of us if I were to try to carry on now. Anyhow, though Mary wouldn't play me a dirty trick—not that kind, at least—the theater won't have any part of me. They're all backing her in this marital fracas. So I am looking around for a new and fruitful field for my peculiar talents."

"I saw Mary half an hour ago."

"You did!" Tom's face darkened. "You didn't waste any time."

"Don't be such an idiot! She saw by the paper that I was back and she dropped in to say hello. She didn't even come upstairs. Not five minutes in all, most decorously spent down in the lobby under the eyes of the doorman."

"Sorry." Tom had the grace to look ashamed. "I guess I'm raw on the subject of Mary." He raised his empty glass. "Any more of this? My favorite brew. I call it marriage—on the rocks."

Vic was not sympathetic. "Get what you want, but stop dramatizing yourself."

Tom spoke from the kitchen as though it were easier to talk when they were not face to face. "Are you going to see her again?"

"Tomorrow. Tea at five. Her place."

"Look, Vic, tell her—give her my love, will you?"

"Wouldn't that come better from you?"

Tom appeared in the kitchen doorway. With his wild spirits reined in or damped down he looked curiously defeated. His shoulders slumped. His eyes were sunken. Then he smiled, his black brows lifting slightly at the inner side, giving his face a questioning, deprecating look. It was a boyish expression, revealing a certain weakness, as though he still relied on a disarmingly youthful quality that he should long since have outgrown. True, it had always been Mary who supplied the drive for them both.

"She's finished with me, Vic. All through."

"Why?" Vic asked bluntly. "I thought you two were a team that could weather anything."

"So did I. I'm as crazy about her now as I ever was. Losing her is like losing an arm. I'm crippled without her. It wasn't my fault, Vic. It wasn't her fault. It's that . . ." He fought for control, said tonelessly, "Markham."

"I don't know a more thankless task than offering unsolicited advice," Vic said. "But for the record, I'd like to speak my piece."

"Go ahead."

"Mary, as both Bill and I, as countless other men have found out, never looked twice at anyone but you. She was as deeply in love with you as you are with her."

"But I tell you—"

"I'm telling you. Save it for later. If we're still speaking then. You're touchy, Tom. You and Bill and Mary and I had an unusual relationship, a fine relationship, when you stop to look at the picture —three men in love with one woman, and yet never a moment of tension or doubt. Not on anyone's part."

"Never quite on an equality though," Tom pointed out. "Bill had all the Benton money. You were famous before you were twenty. Mary has been a fabulous success for six years. If Mary's given me up in disgust, who can blame her?" He laughed at himself. "I guess I do. Though . . ."

"Let's keep the scales balanced," Vic said. "Bill had money, I had a career. But you have Mary."

"I had Mary." Tom tipped back the glass, drained it, turned to get a refill.

"Watch it," Vic said. "One more and you're going to be out like a light."

"That's what I'm aiming to do."

"And how do you expect to get out of here in one piece?"

"Oh," Tom said in a tone of surprise, "I'm staying with you."

"The hell you are."

"Matter of fact, there's no place else to go. I got put out today for nonpayment of rent. Tomorrow I'll call on Case to collect my inheritance. He wrote me that Bill's estate has been settled. Right now I'm on the town."

"Okay. You can order food from the restaurant downstairs. I'm going out to dinner."

"On the prowl already?" Tom smiled, but the bloodshot eyes were searching.

The poor fool, Vic thought with a stab of pity. "I'm going to have dinner with the Fedders. The lady telephoned while Miss Manning was here. Asked us both."

"The Chuck Fedders and Helen Manning? Watch your step, boy."

"You know them?"

"Slightly. I saw the Manning girl a couple of times after I came back to New York. She's taken on Brenda's job with Chuck Fedder, you know."

Vic whistled. "No, she didn't tell me. What do you think of her?"

"Beautiful, if you like statues. An IBM machine dressed by Mainbocher. Very tricky piece of work."

"Tricky?"

"Slipping in questions when she thinks you're loaded and can't guard your tongue."

"What about?" Vic knew he had spoken too quickly, but Tom would hardly notice in his condition.

"About Bill. About you."

"Me?"

42   SCARED TO DEATH

Tom grinned. "You," he repeated softly. "Take care of yourself, pal."

Someone else had warned him to take care of himself. Then he remembered. Mary, of course, in the card that had accompanied her roses.

"That's what I do best. Anyhow, it will give me an incentive to walk back across the park. If I don't get enough exercise, my leg stiffens up."

"I thought you'd had your workout for the day."

Vic began to laugh. "I haven't even started."

## FIVE

THE FEDDERS occupied a monstrous apartment on Central Park West with a three-story living room and windows that provided a panoramic view of the park and Fifth Avenue. Public relations must pay off, Vic thought, as he looked at the lavish furnishings, the Picassos and Toulouse-Lautrecs on the walls. He didn't happen to like Toulouse-Lautrec, but he knew that these pictures meant big money. He was glad that he had put on a dinner jacket. It would be expected.

In spite of Bill's comments about Fedder, which he had written off largely to prejudice, he was startled by the first sight of his host when he walked, or waddled, into the room, looking like a penguin in his dinner jacket. He was ovoid, enormous across the hips and tapering to small feet. He was not fat; he was obese, with a face as gross as his body and hands with fingers like sausages. Soft hands that clung like rubber gloves.

Fedder didn't talk; he bellowed. "Wales! Well, this is a pleasure and a privilege. The famous Victor Wales!" He chuckled, shaking his soft belly. There was a roll of fat where his neck should have been. His ears were set in bulges of fat. Small eyes looked out of pouches of fat. "At one time I hated the sound of your name. Know what I mean?"

"Mine?" Vic did not attempt to conceal his astonishment.

"Julie, my wife, heard you in a concert at Carnegie Hall and came home dithering. Not just the music; I could have stood that, though I can take music or leave it alone. Give me some simple folk music or a guitar. That's my speed. But Julie's artistic."

Vic winced but made no comment. The longest and certainly the dullest hours of his life had been spent in listening to people tell him how they felt about music.

"Yeah, she dithered. Not just the music. It was you. A great big hunk of beautiful man."

There wasn't, Vic reflected in distaste, any possible reply to that. But he could take just about one more hint as to his alleged sex life and someone was going to get popped, but good. Then he grinned rather sourly. Last time he had obeyed that impulse he had broken his hand.

Fedder's soft chuckle stopped abruptly. His eyebrows and lips drooped as though he were about to cry. He patted Vic's arm, looking with open curiosity at the ugly scar across the back of his right hand.

"Now they tell me you don't play any more. A great shame."

Vic made no reply.

"An accident?"

"A fight."

"Mr. Wales!" She came into the room on a wave of Chanel Number Five, a tall, lush woman, probably forty but making a gallant struggle to be thirty and nearly succeeding. Her blond hair had received a good deal of assistance. She was, Vic thought, quite a dish. She was, in fact, the kind of woman with whom he usually spent his leisure hours, though he preferred them younger. About fifteen years younger.

She held out both heavily ringed hands. "This is such a thrill. I can't tell you how much I've looked forward to knowing you." Her hands pressed his.

Fedder chuckled. "You don't need to tell him, darling. I already have. My wife, Mr. Wales." No one could mistake his pride in the big golden woman who stood at least a head taller than he.

"Chuck, why don't you take Mr. Wales's cane?"

"Thanks"—Vic intervened before the fat fingers could lift it—"I get around better when I have it."

"You poor man," she crooned. "But your leg is improving, isn't it?"

"Oh yes. It's just a question of time now. And patience."

She sat beside him, unnecessarily close because the couch was wide, one bare arm touching his shoulder. "I'll never understand it. Bill Benton of all people. And that he should turn on his best friend. I'm glad Brenda never knew. It would have broken her heart. How on earth did it happen, Mr. Wales? We've all wondered and wondered."

They weren't, Vic reflected, wasting any time. First his hand. Then his leg. It occurred to him that Julie Fedder wasn't the kind of woman to delay, to wait patiently for what she wanted. She was a grabber and a grabber with a lot of practice.

There was a whiff of perfume, some light flower scent, and Helen Manning appeared. Vic's first impression was that Julie was annoyed by the interruption. His second impression was that he had better revise his ideas about the Manning girl. She wasn't his type, but she might prove a disturbing influence if he permitted her to be.

Her hair was still drawn back, smooth as silk; her skin had a flawless quality, a petal softness and transparency he had never seen in anyone over ten years old. Her evening dress of gray chiffon emphasized the clear gray of her eyes and made apparent just how much she had concealed by the tailored suit.

"Good evening, Mr. Wales." She adroitly avoided shaking hands by taking a chair some distance away from him. "Are you getting settled?"

"Not yet. I haven't even unpacked. I had some company after you left. In fact, I still have. Tom Keith has moved in with me temporarily."

"So it's true that his wife has kicked him out," Julie Fedder said.

Rather ostentatiously Vic made no comment, and for a moment both Fedder and his wife were aware of the awkwardness. Helen Manning did nothing to ease the tension. She sat holding her martini glass and smoking, waiting passively for what might happen. Vic had a vivid picture of her watching the Christian martyrs being turned loose to the lions. He wondered if their first terrors and struggles and screams would wrest so much as a yawn from her.

It was Julie who broke the silence, her rather weary eyes that were so much older than the well-creamed face fixed rather challengingly on Vic.

"Mary's an old friend of yours, isn't she?"

"She and Tom are both old friends of mine."

"But they aren't together now," Julie said. "Whose fault it is I'm sure I don't know, though I hear things." She looked at Vic who did not ask her what things she heard. "In fact, we're all wondering who the new man is."

Vic was alarmed by his own anger. "I can't believe that of Mary," he said as quietly as he could. He was aware that he had captured Helen Manning's interest. Any reference to Mary seemed to alert her.

"Always men with you, Julie," Fedder said, but his chuckle did not quite come off. "With all women, I suppose."

"That's Chuck," Julie snapped. "Whenever a marriage fails he blames the poor wife, no matter how innocent she may be, no matter what the husband is like."

"Marriage is marriage, if you know what I mean."

"We know what you mean," Julie said wearily. "And I still say, who is Mary looking for now?"

"I don't know who Mary is looking for," Vic said evenly, "but Tom is looking for a job."

"Tom Keith? You're kidding!" Julie exclaimed. "That man doesn't need a job."

"He does now. He's no longer Mary's press agent. He couldn't very well continue as things are."

"He's a terrific press agent," Fedder said thoughtfully. "But terrific. You ask me and I'll tell you he built the image of Mary that made her the public figure she is today. Little things. A touch here, a touch there. Nothing cheap like those old dodges of pretending their jewelry was stolen so as to get a story in the papers. Nope, he created that warm, human, unspoiled image."

"She was like that before she married Tom," Vic said.

Chuck brushed this aside, afire with a new idea. "If he's serious about a job, I'll take him on tomorrow. Tell him that, will you, Wales? I'm working on a stunt now that he'd go for in a big way." His soft body shook with his laugh.

Julie groaned. "The sixteen blondes?"

"The sixteen blondes. Take a guy like Tom Keith. With his flair he'd get those blondes on television as legitimate news. He'd have 'em in *Life*. He'd make them the talk of the town. You tell him to give me a ring and I'll fix him up, and the sooner the better."

"He wouldn't fit into the organization, Chuck," his wife protested. "He was good. Okay, he was good. But he's hitting the sauce lately. Every bar in town."

"How many have you been in?"

For a moment husband and wife exchanged a look that revealed, Vic thought, their conjugal pattern. Chuck was infatuated with his wife and ridden with jealousy, which was probably justified. Julie made no attempt to conceal her contempt. She was too sure of him to need to bother.

She shrugged. "You tell him, Helen. Keith is simply not the right man for us."

"I barely know him," Helen said indifferently. Her cool eyes swept over Vic's face. "I'm afraid you were disturbed by the evening paper, Mr. Wales."

"And small wonder if he was," Julie exclaimed, warmly partisan. "Just because he came into all that money! Why shouldn't Benton leave it to him? Brenda was dead." She laid a hand heavy with rings on his scarred one. "What did he tell you about her, Mr. Wales? How did he account for her?"

"Dinner is served," the houseman said, and for the second time Julie was annoyed by an interruption.

II

The dinner was a gastronomic triumph, but the ordeal of watching Chuck eat destroyed Vic's appetite. The man's table manners were not offensive, but his gluttony was obscene. Absorbed in his food, he was oblivious to his wife's cold distaste. Only Helen seemed to be impervious, though she was not, Vic believed, an insensitive person.

He made no effort to guide the conversation, forcing the Fedders to take the lead. As Chuck had no interest in anything but his food, this left the initiative to Julie. Helen remained blandly passive.

"And what," Julie demanded vivaciously, "are you planning to do?"

"Just take it easy for a while. Enjoy New York. See some plays. It's years since I've had any real leisure."

"Of course, all those concert tours. They must have been exhausting. How wonderful not to have to work any more."

There was no possible answer to that. Vic set down his fork carefully, managing to keep his face expressionless. But Julie's remark did have the effect of stirring Helen Manning into speech, as though she, too, had experienced a shock at the blundering words. For the rest of the meal she kept the conversation assiduously on the New York theater.

"Let's have coffee in the living room," Julie suggested at the end of what had begun to seem like an interminable meal. "And you, Victor—I have to call you that; I feel we are going to be real friends—must rest your poor leg. Does it cause you a great deal of pain?"

"Not really. Now and then, of course, if I overdo."

"Was he crazy?" Julie demanded. "I know I shouldn't say it, but after all, how else can we account for Bill Benton shooting you and killing himself?"

"How else?" Vic said noncommittally.

"You knew dear Brenda, too, didn't you?"

"From the time she was ten years old."

"Was she always such an odd little creature? I don't mean," Julie said hastily, "that we didn't love her. But we couldn't help wondering—did she tell Bill why she acted as she did?"

"You mean when she refused to testify?"

"Yes. You see, Victor, she seemed like such a nice girl, but she caused Chuck and me terrible embarrassment. After all, Chuck was entirely in the clear on that Markham business. There wasn't anything she could have said. He had nothing to do with that deal. But Brenda let people believe she was concealing something. She did us no service, I can tell you that!"

"Still no evidence ever came out that could do you any real damage," Vic said.

"It wasn't evidence," Chuck put in. "It was rumors. That was the whole trouble. Nothing to get hold of. Rumors destroyed Markham. Rumors made people believe Ralston's contract wasn't on the up and up. Rumors pointed to me and my outfit."

"Who started the rumors?"

"There you have me," Chuck admitted. "No one ever found out."

"Did you know this man Ralston who got the contract? Army clothing, wasn't it?"

Chuck lumbered across the room and busied himself pouring brandy. It was Julie who said, "Why, of course we know him. He was one of Chuck's clients. But Chuck had no hand in swinging that government contract. Chuck doesn't even know anyone on the purchasing committee. He never heard of it until the story hit the papers."

"Never knew a thing about it," Chuck said, coming back with a tray of glasses. "I work hard. I do crazy things. Know what I mean? That's part of the racket. But I've never been crooked." He spread a fat hand on his chest. "They crucified me. Crucified me. And me with a record like an unborn babe. You can tell him, Helen. Ever seen anything wrong in the way I do business?"

"Not a thing," she said sleepily.

"And Brenda didn't either," Julie said. "So why didn't she speak out? There must have been a reason. Victor, I simply can't believe she didn't say something to her brother."

Vic made no comment.

"But what did he tell you? What do you know?" Three pairs of eyes searched Vic's unrevealing face.

"He talked chiefly about her death. You were there at the time, weren't you?"

Chuck handed around the brandy glasses. "Sure. It was the poor kid's birthday. Mary Smith gave the party."

"Did you see it happen?"

Chuck shook his head. "After lunch I took a nap, fell asleep on the beach. So far as I know, Brenda was the only one who went in swimming, and you know how it is at Mary's—just that one narrow strip of beach and then the shore line bends and you can't see beyond that."

"That's odd. Looks as though she walked out on

her own party." Vic noticed that Helen was looking at him thoughtfully over her brandy snifter.

"She was embarrassed," Julie explained. "John Markham was there. Of course." She let the words stand in isolation for a moment. "Then Horace Ralston drifted over from his place to say hello to Mary. So Brenda went in swimming."

"That must have been quite a situation, Ralston and Markham having the grand confrontation."

"Julie took care of Ralston," Chuck said tartly. "Dragged him away from the others."

"I was only trying to ease the situation," she defended herself.

"It seems odd to think of Mary without Tom," Vic said.

"Oh, Tom showed up. But when he saw Markham he cleared out."

The conversation dropped. Vic made no effort to keep it going. Then Julie said abruptly, "Victor, what did Bill think? About Brenda, I mean."

"He thought," Vic told her calmly, "that she was murdered."

## SIX

VIC STROLLED back slowly through Central Park. The lighting was inadequate and the path not easy to follow, but the footsteps on the gravel behind him were clearly audible, even above the roar of traffic on Central Park South and the hum of motors moving through the park itself. Perhaps they would not have been so obvious if he had not been listening for them.

He had anticipated them ever since he had seen Helen Manning put down the telephone in the small study. He wondered whether he should make it simple by sitting down on a bench, but he continued to saunter, his cane gripped in his hand. Something brushed against his coat, and he swung, the cane lashed out, and a man fell headlong. By the dim flame of his pocket lighter Vic looked at him. He wasn't badly hurt, but he had knocked himself out in his fall, a small man with a bald head and a long thin nose. I'll remember you, Vic thought. He went on, hastening his pace, heading for Fifth Avenue and lights and people.

He entered the first well-lighted bar with a sense of escape. After the second drink his leg stopped throbbing. No one appeared to be loitering on the street, but the three blocks to the Beekman Place address seemed endless. He kept away from buildings, walking near the curb, listening for footsteps behind him.

He let himself into the apartment quietly. Tom's door was wide open and Tom, half dressed, was sprawled across the bed he had not bothered to make up. The lights shone down on his face where the shadow of a beard was beginning to appear. He looked young and battered and profoundly unhappy.

Vic eased open the window, pulled a quilt over the sleeping man, switched out the light, and closed the door behind him.

When he had poured himself a nightcap he sank into a comfortable chair in the living room, staring out at the lights of Manhattan and Long Island. Somehow he had not anticipated such swift action or that it would take a violent form. He went over the evening with the Fedders. Chuck he dismissed as of little interest. Julie Fedder was a different proposition. A ruthless woman. A rapacious woman. An unscrupulous woman. But not, he thought, intelligent.

The obese Fedder and his wife were curious associates for Helen Manning. If Fedder hadn't picked his wife up in a bar, Vic would be surprised. Helen was highly intelligent, fastidious, and sensitive. She had shared his shock over Julie's airy dismissal of his career and had prevented her from making any further blunders. But it was Helen, he felt convinced, who had sent the long-nosed man into Central Park. And that was not the way Vic had expected it to be.

In his own bedroom—Brenda's room, he realized—there was none of the feminine clutter that must have been there while she lived, but it was unmistakably a woman's room. The pictures on the walls were photographs that she wanted around her: Bill at all ages, Tom, David Case, himself, John Markham. Odd, there was no picture of Mary who, for so long, had been a part of that small circle.

Vic unpacked his bags and stowed away his clothes in the closet, feeling like an intruder. The bed had been freshly made up. When he had undressed and put on pajamas and dressing gown, he prowled restlessly, unable, in spite of his fatigue, to sleep. Under the window there were several shelves of books, and he bent over to examine them.

It was a curious assortment, made up of standard volumes of poetry, most of them dating back to the nineteenth century, love stories that were unabashedly sentimental, and a recent series of biographies and autobiographies of politicians and statesmen, gaudy in their bright jackets.

Who, he wondered, had stirred Brenda's interest in contemporary politics? The charming but ambiguous John Markham? There was Markham's own book, *In the Public Interest,* a title that had occasioned a good deal of satirical comment at the peak of the scandal. An inscription read: "For Brenda who understands."

One by one, Vic removed the books, shook them, looking for loose papers. Nothing fell out except a card reminding Brenda of a dental appointment, a card which she had used as a bookmark. He found himself wondering irrelevantly whether she had kept the appointment.

It was in a worn copy of Wordsworth that he discovered the underlined passage:

Why art thou silent! . . .
Is there no debt to pay, no boon to grant?
Yet have my thoughts for thee been vigilant,
Bound to thy service with unceasing care . . .
Speak that my torturing doubts their end may know!

In spite of his fatigue he found it difficult to sleep. After the quiet of Wyoming and the total darkness in his hospital room at night he was disturbed by the noise of the great restless city, by the lights that enabled him to distinguish even the colors of the chairs.

He turned restlessly in Brenda's bed, Brenda who would never be restless again.

*Bound to thy service with unceasing care . . .*

How deeply she had loved to be willing to face that committee and remain silent, to endure the knowledge that she had tarnished her reputation. But she had been careful, very careful, not to leave behind any trace of the man's identity. Vic had made sure of that.

*They've tried to kill me.*

Oh God, he thought, and turned his head away from the light, shutting out the sight of Brenda's room, of his own face looking back at him from the wall.

II

Something tinkled in the kitchen sink and Vic was wide-awake immediately. He looked at his watch. Nearly ten o'clock. Was Tom starting his drinking so early?

He pulled on a bathrobe and padded out to the kitchen. A brown-skinned woman, wearing a big apron, was washing out last night's glasses and ash trays. She had a pleasant, low-pitched voice with a British accent.

"Mr. Wales? I am Winnie. Miss Manning said you might want me to stay."

"I'll be glad to have you stay. You know the place and I'm not—at least I hope I'm not—difficult to work for."

Winnie smiled. "Usually men are easier to work for."

"You found Miss Manning difficult?"

"Well, I liked Miss Brenda best." Winnie hesitated. "She was—you know how she was. But Miss Manning—well, she was considerate and always polite but—always snooping."

"Do you think you can get me some coffee?"

"Right away. Bacon and eggs or—"

"Bacon and eggs will be fine. Bacon crisp and the eggs over lightly."

"Yes, sir."

When he had showered, shaved, and dressed, he came out to find a small table set near the window where he could look out on that terrific view. This morning something, perhaps the sunlight, perhaps the heavy sleep into which he had eventually fallen, had driven away the ghosts of the night before. Vic's spirits rose. There was nothing he couldn't handle if he managed to keep his head. As he drank the first cup of excellent coffee his mood of euphoria intensified.

"Have you worked here long, Winnie?" he asked as she refilled his cup and brought a plate of bacon, eggs, and hot buttered toast.

"Five years, sir. Just mornings, of course."

"Then you knew both the Benton twins."

"Yes, sir." Her voice was somber. "Knew them both. The nicest, kindest people I ever worked for. The—gentlest." That had been David Case's word. "When things like that happen to people like that it's hard to tell myself that God sees the sparrow fall. If He does, why couldn't He have stopped it?"

He looked up to find her eyes steady on his, to observe the intelligence in them. "I forgot to tell you, Winnie, I have a guest staying with me. Mr.

Keith. He's—a bit under the weather, so he will probably sleep late this morning."

"Mr. Tom Keith?"

"You know him too?"

"Oh yes. He's an old friend of the family. Always in and out as though it were his own home."

"Morning, Winnie." Tom appeared in the door of his room. "Vic, may I borrow your razor?"

"Go ahead. How about some breakfast?"

Tom shuddered. "Don't use obscene words, but I could drink about a gallon of coffee."

While Winnie brought coffee Tom dragged up another chair to the table. He rubbed his hand through his tousled hair.

"Now where did I leave my suitcases?" he wondered aloud. "This suit needs pressing and I'll have to have a clean shirt. Oh, I remember. Shoved them in a locker at Grand Central. If I don't do some renovating before I barge into Case's office, I'll look more like a man seeking a handout than one coming in to claim his legitimate inheritance."

"By the way, there's a job in the offing if you want it." Vic told him about Fedder's suggestion.

"Chuck Fedder," Tom said thoughtfully. "Well, what do you know? Not exactly my field, but—" He refilled his cup and lighted a cigarette. There was a slight tremor in his fingers. "The wages of sin are catching up on me. If I'm going to earn an honest penny, I had better go back on the wagon."

"You're going to take Fedder up on this offer then?" Vic was surprised.

"Beggars can't be choosers. At least I can find out what it's all about."

"Do you know him well?"

"I've met both Chuck and the fair Julie because they were fairly close to Brenda. And Julie, in case you didn't guess it last night, is the brains behind that outfit."

"As the result of the lessons of a misspent life,"

Vic commented, "I wouldn't have said it was brains that put her ahead of the game."

"She may have her little flings," Tom agreed, "but he's jealous. If she slipped up and he caught her at it, he could be very nasty."

"They went to Brenda's birthday party, didn't they? Why didn't you tell Bill you were on hand when she was drowned?"

Tom looked helpless. "I tried to talk about her, time after time, but he clammed up. And he was so shattered by the whole thing I couldn't see that it would help matters to tell him I saw her the very day she died, though, as a matter of fact, I wasn't there when she went in swimming. I just dropped by to bring some champagne because we always have celebrated birthdays together. Anyhow"—he gave Vic a wry look—"I thought it would be an excuse to see Mary, to find out if she had changed, to figure out if I had a chance. Then that—then Markham came strolling along the beach, acting as though he belonged there, which he probably does, so I cleared out."

He changed the subject abruptly. "I didn't hear you come in. Passed out somewhere along the line." He grinned. "As you must have noticed. Someone seems to have tucked me in for the night."

"I tangled with a mugger in the park. They ought to police that place better. I felt safer in the Rockies than I do in Manhattan."

"What happened?"

Vic grinned. "He fell over my cane and knocked himself out."

"And then what? Did you call a cop?"

"If there was one in the park, he was hiding behind a tree. I left him to come to at his leisure."

Tom laughed. "You're a ruthless son of a gun. Have a pleasant evening otherwise?"

"If watching Chuck Fedder eat can be called pleasant," Vic said with a wince of disgust.

"Quite an operation," Tom agreed. "They do these

things so much better in pigpens. I suppose our fair Julie was making an early bid for part of that lovely money of yours. Of the two I'd take Chuck any day. Julie's more apt to take you. Her share-the-wealth campaign. If it's your wealth."

"She didn't strike me as needing a handout. Not in that apartment. And she was plastered with diamonds."

"Well"—Tom pushed back from the table—"I'd better go salvage my wardrobe and prepare to meet the mighty man on his own ground. One thing about his office, you never know what you'll find. Once, so help me, it was a snake charmer complete with snake. Today it may be tame crocodiles."

"Today," Vic said, "it's more apt to be sixteen blondes, but whether tame or not I can't say."

"You cheer me. You brighten my day. See you for dinner?"

Vic hesitated. "I'm not sure of my plans. Better leave it open."

III

Mary Smith still lived in a suite high up in an apartment hotel on Central Park South. She came to the door wearing black velvet slacks and a white satin blouse.

"Vic, darling!" She flung herself into his arms and kissed him exuberantly. Then she held him back to look at him. That, of course, was part of the secret of her enormous popularity. Even across the footlights she gave people the impression that she was entirely engrossed in them. Her personal warmth and friendliness touched them like a soft breeze.

She drew him down beside her on the big chesterfield that looked out on a long vista of Central Park. As usual, the living room was untidy. A script had been thrown down on a coffee table. Music scores spilled off the piano. A sweater with, he was prepared to swear, a large hole in it lay across a chair.

"You look better today. How did you spend your first evening home, or is it anything you can tell me?"

Vic shook his head more in anger than in sorrow. "Where I got this reputation as a tomcat I can't imagine. But I actually spent the evening most respectably with the Chuck Fedders."

Mary shivered. "That revolting couple. I didn't know you had ever met them."

"I hadn't. They called and asked me to dinner."

"But why on earth—oh, don't laugh. I know all about your attraction for women."

"Except you."

"Except me." She smiled. "But to ask a stranger . . ."

"Their mutual friend, as Dickens had it. They knew the Bentons. I knew the Bentons. At once we find a bond."

"Was that man Ralston there too?"

"No, the only other guest was Helen Manning."

"How could you bear to spend an evening with them?"

"They seemed to be very friendly. And it paid off. They are going to give Tom a job. I suppose you know he's on his uppers, kicked out of his apartment for nonpayment of rent."

"No!" She was incredulous.

"Right now he's staying with me at the apartment. Fedder jumped at the chance to get him."

"But surely Tom wouldn't work for a man like that! Even if he is as broke as you think he is, and I don't see how that's possible."

"A job is a job is a job."

"That isn't funny. Not funny at all. The Fedders were back of the Ralston deal. Tom would know that. He's only doing this because—"

"Because it would annoy?"

She didn't answer. She got up to fix drinks. They wouldn't want tea, she said; they needed something more fortifying. Everything—bottles, glasses, ice—had been set out on a long table against the wall, but it took her a long time to prepare two glasses of bourbon and water.

Vic sat with one hand balancing his cane, moving it backward and forward, watching her gravely. "What went wrong, Mary? Tom is breaking his heart. I thought that marriage was made for keeps."

"So did I." The deep, thrilling tone was in her voice. She came back to hand him a glass and sink onto the chesterfield beside him. "Is he still drinking himself blind?"

"He's making an impressive effort in that direction."

"Did he drink that much while he was out in the Rockies with you and Bill?"

"Yes."

"Vic"—an oddly blunt hand caught at his sleeve—"what happened out there?"

"I thought the papers carried the whole story."

"Did they?"

His hand tightened on the cane. "What do you want to know?"

"According to the news stories, Bill went berserk, shot you, and killed himself."

"Well?"

"I don't believe it," Mary said quietly.

## SEVEN

THE HAND THAT had been moving the cane became motionless. It seemed to Vic that the very air in the room was heavy to breathe.

Mary forced herself to look at him. Her face was ravaged. There was nothing glamorous about her now. Even the slim body seemed to have thickened, to be collapsing instead of being held with the grace that had long controlled her movements.

"There were no actual witnesses, were there? That is, the Forest Rangers were near enough to hear the shots but not near enough to see the shooting. And Tom was out gathering firewood."

"I see." There was no change in his expression that she could discern. "And why do you think I shot Bill, Mary? Oh, of course, the inheritance plus the fact that I am known as Vic the Violent."

She sat drawing a design on the carpet with the toe of her slipper. "But you do have a quick temper. How did you break your hand, Vic?"

"In a fight. In a bar."

"What would make you angry enough to take a terrible chance like that?"

There was a tap at the door and she said in exasperation, "People aren't supposed to be sent up without being announced."

The man in the doorway said, "Mary, I've got to see you."

Her voice, sharp with suspicion when she had spoken to Vic, warmed with concern. "John, my dear, what's happened?"

"I can't take any more." He broke off as he caught sight of Vic. The latter recognized him at once, though he was in many ways unlike the John Markham whose picture he had studied the day before. He looked ten years older, his hair was dusted with gray, his face was lined; a man pursued by the Furies and too exhausted for further flight.

"Vic," Mary said, "this is John Markham. Victor Wales."

The two men murmured something polite, but they did not shake hands. Markham, who obviously had not been prepared to find another caller, hovered without sitting down. He refused a drink.

"I can't stay. Just dropped in for a minute."

Vic reached for his glass, looked at the scar across the back of his hand, and laughed.

"What's the joke?" Mary demanded.

"You were asking about my hand. You know,

that's a funny thing, Mary. A very funny thing. Some guy came into this bar and started talking about you. He'd seen you the night before in *Slim Rations*. He said you were known to be two-timing Tom. I was so mad I smashed my hand in an all-out scrap with him. Amusing, isn't it?"

For a moment he thought she was going to be sick. At the same time he thought Markham was going to jump him. He watched them both with detached curiosity, one hand gripping his stick.

Then when he discovered that Mary was not going to say anything, he remarked, "Fair's fair. You asked about Bill. Suppose you tell me about Brenda."

Markham stirred, then forced himself to be still. Mary's mouth, which had grown slack under the shock of his statement about his hand, hardened.

"I don't know, Vic. I've never figured her out. I used to be fond of the Bentons. They were Tom's friends, and in those days his friends were mine. But when she stood before that committee and refused to say a word that might have cleared John, I—hated her. How could she have done it? So cruel, so vicious a thing. How could she?"

*I can't help it, Bill.*

"Of course," he said lazily, "if she knew Markham was innocent, she should have said so." His eyes met those of Markham in a long, steady look.

Even now, his face fine-drawn from his long ordeal, his expression one of unutterable weariness, Markham had the unmistakable patina of the man of destiny. That presidents had trusted his judgment, that a nation had believed in his integrity, was easy to understand. What baffled the understanding was that he could have been toppled from his position or, if rumor was true, had stooped to dishonor.

"That has been the sixty-four-dollar question all along," Markham said wearily. "Did you ever try to fight a rumor, to pin down a smoke ring, to nail a bit of fog? It's a particularly frustrating business. You exhaust yourself and you get nowhere."

"Of course John was innocent," Mary said impatiently. "And yet Brenda helped to wreck his life. Did it deliberately. Sometimes I think drowning was too good for her."

Whether it was her warm partisanship or something else, Vic's sympathy ebbed. "Still it was probably the best that could be done at the time."

It was a moment before his meaning registered. "What do you mean by that?"

*Find out whom she was protecting and then, by God, you'll find out who murdered her.*

"Where were you and Markham when Brenda went swimming?"

"John and I? Why, I don't know. What are you trying to say?"

"Bill thought Brenda was murdered, Mary. So do I now. So that, whatever she knew or suspected, she would never be able to speak."

Mary looked at him but she did not see him; she leaned forward slowly and toppled onto the floor.

II

Tom was in the Beekman Place apartment, shaved, neatly dressed, and cold sober. He was also, as he informed Vic, solvent. Case had turned over the twenty-five thousand dollars Bill had left him and he had deposited the money at once.

"The cashier nearly fainted. I usually take money out."

Vic looked him over. "I should think that would call for a celebration, but it doesn't seem to be working that way."

Tom avoided his eyes. "Case and I had quite a talk. About this and that."

Vic eased himself into a chair, his eyes still on Tom's face.

"And?"

"He probably shouldn't have told me—professional

confidence and all that—but he said you'd made a will leaving everything to Mary."

"And?" Vic repeated.

"Is it too much to ask—why?"

"Suppose," Vic said pleasantly, "you figure that one out for yourself."

Tom walked to the window, stared out, his back to the room.

After an interval Vic asked, "What about the Fedder deal?"

"I got the job. Crazy as a loon, the way that guy does business, but it seems to pay off. Now I'll look around for a place to live."

"You can stay on here until you find what you like."

At last Tom turned back from the window. "Thanks," he said awkwardly. "That's very decent of you. I won't be in the way?"

"You'll have the place to yourself. I'm going up to the country tonight."

"Connecticut?"

"Yes."

"By the way, this came for the Manning girl today." Tom indicated a box with the address of a Fifth Avenue store. "Know where she went?"

Vic picked up a card that had been stuck in the corner of the blotter on the small desk. "Here's her address. I'll take care of this."

"What are you up to, Vic?"

Vic grinned. "I don't believe in letting a good thing go by default. I think I'll deliver this box myself."

"I don't mean that, as you know damned well. What was the idea of telling the Fedders last night that you thought Brenda had been murdered?"

"I said Bill thought so."

"They were stunned. Where in hell did Bill get such an idea? Or did he really lose his marbles that last day?"

"Brenda wrote him that someone had tried to kill

her. She was genuinely terrified and wanted him to come back."

"Good God! There was never the slightest suggestion of anything but accident. What do you believe, Vic?"

"I'm keeping an open mind."

"It seems so rotten to stir up the whole thing again. I wish we could let that poor, pathetic kid rest. She deserved that much from us. She didn't really get much out of life, you know, in spite of all that money, except a lot of romantic dreams."

Vic shrugged and went to his room to pack a bag.

"Did you see Mary?" Tom raised his voice so Vic could hear.

"I just came from there."

"How was she?"

Vic remembered Mary's gray face as she toppled onto the carpet. "Fine. Just fine. I gave her your message."

"Did she say anything?" Tom asked eagerly.

"She asked whether you were still drinking yourself to death."

"Oh." Tom managed an unconvincing laugh. "That doesn't sound very encouraging, does it?"

"I've never believed in the efficacy of a Miles Standish courtship. If you want to plead your cause, you'll have to speak for yourself."

"But I can't get within shouting distance! Did you tell her Bill thought Brenda had been murdered?"

"Mary hates Brenda's guts."

"She does?" Tom was startled. "Mary? I can't believe it. She never hates anyone."

"Well, she does. Even now. Even when Brenda is dead and silenced. She thinks Brenda could have cleared Markham." Vic came back into the living room with his suitcase.

"It's the hell of a thing," Tom said slowly. "You know, I've always thought that Brenda, too, was in love with Markham. That's why she kept still. She wouldn't lie, but she wouldn't betray him either. It's funny, isn't it, that Mary can't see the truth about that man. Maybe Brenda did swim out too far. On purpose. Killed herself as Bill killed himself. Markham has a lot to answer for, Vic. Some day he will pay for what he has done."

"Markham," Vic pointed out, "is already paying. His career is a thing of shreds and patches, in case you hadn't noticed."

"He isn't paying enough. Not half enough. What is it about him that blinds women, dazzles them? The knight-in-armor stuff? Sir Lancelot?"

"Lancelot, as I remember, got himself in a bit of trouble over women," Vic reminded him. He called the garage and asked to have the Benton car brought around.

"Do the Ellises know that you're going up to the Connecticut house?"

"No."

"They'll stand by for invasion. That's fair warning. They'll probably throw pails of boiling water out of the window. They are gunning for you, boy."

Vic laughed. "Then they are in good company and plenty of it."

"They wanted to break Bill's will. Undue influence. And I might say," Tom added, "that young Case practically suggested it. At least he didn't discourage the idea."

"Did he, indeed? I was aware of a certain atmosphere of no enthusiasm when I met him." Vic picked up the suitcase, tucked the dress box under his arm. "Be seeing you."

The car was a fairly new Chrysler and a joy to handle. Vic drove west to Fifth Avenue and then headed south. At Tenth Street he turned west again, driving slowly, and looking at numbers. The one he wanted must be across the street. He pulled in at the curb and shut off the motor.

The number he sought was over the door of an old-fashioned apartment building. At the entrance two people were talking: a slim woman, hatless, her dark hair smooth as silk, wearing a dramatic cape of Chinese red lined with fur. The man to whom she was speaking so earnestly was no taller than she and had a bald head and a long nose. The last time Vic had seen him he was lying unconscious on a gravel path in Central Park. As Vic watched them, the man turned and walked briskly away, the woman disappeared inside the building.

Vic sat back and smoked a cigarette slowly. Then he crushed it in the ash tray, picked up the box, and got out to lock the car. There was a long, narrow lobby with paint peeling off the ceiling and an inadequate droplight. Along the wall was a row of bells with cards over them. An arrow pointed to the elevator. A second arrow was marked "A." He followed it through a doorway at the back and walked across a dark garden, following a dim flagged path.

Fifty feet back he saw the dark outlines of the house. It was larger than he had expected, a two-story frame structure. An English carriage lamp lighted the heavy oak door with its ornate knocker.

He hammered loudly. In a few moments high heels clicked rapidly across the floor and the door was opened.

"Mr. Wales!" She was startled.

"Good evening, Miss Manning. This was delivered at the apartment for you while I was out this afternoon. I thought I would bring it down myself in case it was something you wanted immediately."

"How nice of you." She took the box, hesitated, and then stepped back. "Won't you come in? Perhaps you'll have a drink with me."

"That would be pleasant." For a moment he looked appreciatively around the room, a two-story studio with an enormous fireplace, bookshelves reaching to the ceiling, even crossing the mantel, with a bright-painted ladder swinging from the toprail. Half of the ceiling was a skylight. In one corner a circular staircase rose to the second floor. There were deep couches, comfortable chairs, lamps that spilled a soft glow on mellow oriental rugs.

"What luck to find this!" he exclaimed.

"Wasn't it?"

While she busied herself in the kitchen he prowled around the room, skimming over titles of books, pausing before an easel to inspect the oil painting on it, a curious abstract design. He glanced toward the kitchen and then reached out a cautious finger and touched the paint. He stood leaning on his cane, whistling the opening theme of the Archduke trio.

There was a tinkle of ice and she came in with a tray containing a pitcher of martinis and two chilled cocktail glasses.

"That's a pleasant sound," he said.

"So is the Archduke. You used to play a lot of chamber music, didn't you?"

He nodded and came to seat himself beside the cocktail table.

"Why? You were such a terrific success. Why did you subordinate yourself to others?"

"Not to others. To music. Some of the most beautiful music is in the trios and quartets and quintets." He was impatient. He had never liked discussing music except with musicians. Now it was unbearable to discuss it at all.

"It's such a beastly shame!" she burst out. "Such a waste!"

When the sickness receded he reached for the glass she handed him. Over the rim he looked at her, a provocative gleam in his eyes. "To our future."

She deliberately set down her glass untouched.

"Then suppose," he suggested, "you supply your own toast."

"I'm not good at toasts."

"What is your specialty?" He glanced at the canvas on the easel. "Your work?" When she did not answer he said gently, "The paint is still damp."

"My work," she admitted. "Just a hobby."

"What does it mean? It looks confused to me."

"It isn't really, once you understand the pattern."

He grinned at her. "I'm beginning to."

She sat holding her glass, a poised, relaxed woman; a beautiful woman if you like them made of glass and steel.

"Mr. Wales, why did you tell the Fedders last night that Brenda had been murdered? That was a terrible thing to say."

"It was a terrible thing to happen. You were there, Miss Manning. You shared an apartment with her. You saw her day after day. Didn't you know something was wrong?"

"Of course I knew something was wrong. The poor girl was desperately unhappy."

"Why didn't she tell the committee the truth? She was an innately honest person, a loyal person. Why did she behave as she did?"

"I don't know."

"I assume you are convinced that Fedder was in the clear on the Ralston-Markham deal or you wouldn't be working for him."

"He pays well," she said without expression. "But to go back to this—accusation. I still can't understand it. There was absolutely no suggestion at the time that she had been killed. She went in swimming alone. There was no one with her. The thing is impossible."

"Her last letter to Bill said that someone had tried to kill her and that she was terrified. Her actual words were, 'Scared to death.' Was she, Miss Manning?"

The clear cool gray eyes stared at him and they might have been blind.

"How did they find her?"

"When she didn't come back, Mary called the Coast Guard. They spotted her." As the knocker banged she started, spilling her drink. She went quickly to answer the noisy summons.

"Horace!" she exclaimed, and she was not pleased.

She stepped outside, and Vic could hear muffled voices. Now, he thought, I'll have seen the whole cast. Then she opened the door and admitted a big florid man of fifty who had the dominant air of a successful executive.

"Mr. Wales," she said, "Mr. Ralston."

Ralston shook hands, removed hat and overcoat, and looked around, apparently very much at home. Helen Manning did not resume her seat and after a moment Vic took his leave.

She strolled across the dark garden with him to the front door of the apartment house, as a kind of compensation for her abrupt dismissal of him.

"Good night, Mr. Wales. Thank you for bringing my dress." As he touched his hat and started across the street she said softly, "Take care of yourself."

He did not see the car, which had been running without lights. There was a sudden roar of the motor as it bore down on him. He leaped for the opposite curb and fell sprawling over his stick. The car careened down the street, around the corner. There were tapping heels and then Helen was bending over him.

"Mr. Wales! Are you hurt?"

With her help and using the cane for balance, he got to his feet. For a moment he thought his left leg had been broken, but it was only pain from the blow he had given it. Just his luck to strike the place where his shinbone had been shattered.

He was breathing hard, but he grinned at her. "Two runs and two misses, but no hits so far. Well, if at first you don't succeed . . ."

He unlocked the car door, slid under the wheel with difficulty, hauled in his left leg.

"Wait," she said, "you can't drive like that. Why don't you leave the car here and take a taxi home?"

"I'm going up to the Connecticut house tonight."

"But you can't drive. You aren't fit . . ." She saw the determination in his face. "Then I'm going with you. Wait for me." To make sure he did so she reached in and removed the key. Then she ran back across the street.

Once the agony in his leg had subsided, Vic leaned back in the seat, groping for a cigarette. He pressed in the lighter. The pattern, he said, was beginning to be clear. But was it? Two attempts to kill him. What had sparked them? Undoubtedly his accusation that Brenda Benton had been murdered. His arrival in New York seemed to have set off an alarm system.

At the moment he did not feel that any insurance company would be optimistic about his life expectancy. On the other hand, he was still in the driver's seat as he had intended to be. He looked down at the lock from which Helen Manning had removed the key. Or was he? Was that a symbolic action?

To change the metaphor, was he forcing the play, as he hoped, or was he following someone else's lead? He took a last pull on the cigarette and jammed it savagely into the ash tray. How else could I have played it, he wondered.

Within ten minutes Helen Manning returned, accompanied by Ralston who was carrying a small week-end case, which he placed on the floor in back. He looked curiously at Vic.

"Understand you had a near accident. You have to watch yourself in New York these days. Thugs all over the place."

"So I've noticed. But we Wales have a strong instinct for survival."

"You may need it." The warning was clear now.

Helen waited for Vic to move over, slid in under the wheel, put her handbag beside her, and turned the key in the switch. As she concentrated on maneuvering the car into traffic, toward the West Side Highway, Vic dropped his hand casually on her bag, felt the small revolver inside.

# EIGHT

HER PROFILE was almost flawless. Vic caught himself staring at it and forced himself to look straight ahead. It would be safer to try establish friendly relations with a barracuda.

Above the George Washington Bridge home-coming traffic thinned out, was reduced to a trickle of the hardy who enjoyed country living enough to spend hours a day in travel.

They had reached the Sawmill Parkway before Helen spoke, while Vic waited, leaving the task of initiating the conversation up to her. He was still shaken by the fall, by the suddenness of the attack. And he was more than perplexed by the girl's determination that he should not visit the Connecticut house alone. He grinned as he recalled the way in which she had removed the key so that he could not drive. The girl thought fast.

"That was a deliberate attempt to run you down," she said. He was surprised to hear the tremor in her voice.

"That was my own impression."

"He was waiting for you. He must have followed you to the Village."

"Or simply found me there."

She refused to pick up the flung gauntlet. "Did you recognize him?"

"Not this time, but I'm sure I could pick him out of a crowd. You see, I had a good look at him last night. By the way, while we're on the subject—and you needn't ask what subject—I've removed your revolver. You are safer with me than I am with you."

The car shot ahead from a sudden pressure on the pedal and then steadied.

"Tell me, Miss Manning, was he reporting to you tonight?"

"You mean Ralston?"

"Nonsense. The man with the long nose. The one who tried to run me down. The one who followed me through the park last night after he got your telephone call. Did he tell you I knocked him out?" He added casually, "Very effective cane this. It's loaded."

Somewhat to his surprise, she made no attempt to deny it. After all, since he had recognized the man who attacked him in the park as the one he had found a short time before in her company, she could hardly do so.

"He didn't try to kill you last night. He was trying to protect you."

Vic laughed. "Now I've heard everything."

"You fool! I'm telling you the truth and you haven't intelligence enough to see it. Of all the arrogant, self-satisfied men, you are the most intolerable! The most conceited. The most . . ."

He leaned back in the seat, shouting with laughter. "You are human," he said in delight. "Actually human. I'd begun to think you had one of those orderly, disciplined minds. A combination of a filing cabinet and a highly efficient switchboard. No temper, no emotion, no weaknesses."

"You prefer women with weaknesses obviously."

"At this point," he said smoothly, "my preferences don't really enter into it, do they?"

She was silent for a moment. "Believe me or not, Mr. Wales, I was telling you the truth. He was there last night to protect you. And in case you have any false ideas, that's what I am doing right now."

"I am deeply moved. Solicitude is almost the last quality I would have expected to arouse in you." He grinned to himself, aware that he was goading her. "May I ask what you are protecting me from?"

"I'm not sure."

"Sure about the potential killer or sure about me?"

"Both."

"What would you like to know, Miss Manning?"

"For one thing—where were you when Brenda Benton was drowned?"

The silence lasted one minute, two, three. "Well, well," he said at last.

"It would be so easy, so clever, to cover your tracks like that."

"So it would," he agreed.

"Where were you?" she repeated.

"I was in Sheridan, Wyoming."

"Alone?"

"Far from it. And now about you. I take it that you were at Mary's party."

"Well?"

"Have you an alibi for the time when Brenda died? Has anyone? Is there a single person you can, of your own knowledge, eliminate?"

He had not expected that she would bother to answer. Instead, she seemed to be considering his question.

"I don't know," she said at last. "We split up. The situation was awkward, to say the least. Markham was simply furious when he met Horace Ralston there. I thought—everyone thought—there was going to be trouble. But Mary swept Markham away to look at her new bathhouse and Julie Fedder took charge of Ralston. Chuck fell asleep on the beach, as he said."

"You saw him all the time?"

"I didn't watch him. But he wasn't wearing a bathing suit and he couldn't have gone into the water fully clothed. The Ellises, mother and daughter, were there, but I didn't notice them much. No one would. They were born to be background figures. Anyhow, David Case, with his usual social tact, looked after them."

"What about Tom Keith?"

"He brought some champagne, the ostensible idea being to celebrate Brenda's birthday, but I suspect he was trying to get back into his wife's good graces." Any mention of Mary brought acid into her voice.

"And he failed?"

"Well," she said slowly, "after all, Markham was there. Miss Smith wasn't particularly pleased to have her husband arrive. He was very much the outsider."

"And how about your friend Ralston? He seemed quite at home in your little house tonight."

He half expected her to deny that the house was hers, though it was stamped with her personality. Instead she said, "He did, didn't he? But make no mistake about it, Mr. Wales, entertaining Mr. Ralston, who is one of Chuck's clients, is simply part of my job."

"A pleasant part, I hope."

She made no answer.

II

The restaurant, at the end of a side road, was unexpectedly attractive. When they had ordered, they scrutinized each other straightforwardly. After the curious conversation of the past hour they could hardly regard each other as strangers. Enemies, yes. But they smiled and raised their glasses. This time Vic offered no toast.

Aside from a rather noisy party of six there were only four tables occupied, widely scattered in the big dining room. When Vic passed the basket of hot rolls he caught her eyes resting on his scarred hand. She looked up and blushed deeply.

"I'm sorry it happened," she said. "Bitterly sorry." She sounded as though she meant it.

"It's ancient history."

"It isn't," she said fiercely. "I still think your recording of the Schumann Fantasia is better than the one Horowitz made. It's a revelation. No one who could play like that—"

His hand gripped her wrist, tightening until he hurt her. "Cut it out." His voice was savage. "This happened six months ago. It's the past, the dead past.

When things are over they are over. Let it go, will you?"

The cool gray eyes were on his face and he was aware of what they saw: the bitterness, the frustration, the violence so close to the surface, the submerged pain that could explode into agony when the sore spot was touched. Color flooded her face and then receded slowly.

Vic the Violent, he told himself. He had gone out of his way to offend her; he had deliberately shown her the worst of him. Partly because she was not to be trusted, partly because she was so disturbingly attractive. The gray eyes might be cool, but the perfect lips were warm. Warm and, given the right stimulus, responsive. Cut it out, Wales, he warned himself sharply. You're in enough trouble.

The waiter removed plates, brought others. Vic discovered that he was ravenously hungry. He looked up to comment, "I didn't know I was so hungry. It occurs to me that I've eaten very little in the past forty-eight hours. Chuck's zoo feeding put me off my appetite last night."

When Helen made no reply he said idly, "It's a wonder to me his wife can stand it."

"Julie? I don't suppose she cares very much. Who else could provide her with an apartment like that and the kind of jewelry she wears? In a way I envy her. She's one of the few people who know exactly what they want and who are prepared to pay for it."

"But how much would she pay?" Vic demanded. "Unless I miss my guess, she dominates that outfit. If anyone had a hand in the Ralston contract, my money would be on her."

"I don't know."

"You've been working there how long?"

"Since Brenda died."

"And you don't know what goes on?" he asked skeptically.

She shrugged.

"You take Brenda's job; you share her apartment when you have a perfectly good house of your own. What game are you playing, Helen?"

"I don't know what you mean."

He shook his head, grinning. "You aren't a stupid girl, whatever else you may be. Don't give me that."

The waiter brought dessert and coffee. When he had gone Helen said, "I suppose you know your friend Keith got a job with Chuck today."

"Yes, he told me. It seems rather an odd spot for him, but I hope it will give him something interesting to tie into. He needs an absorbing interest."

"He has one." For the first time Helen laughed and he caught his breath in sheer astonishment. The cold perfection of her face altered, warmed, glowed. She was aware that he was staring at her and something in his eyes informed her of the reason. The laugh broke off as though she were disconcerted.

"You ought to do that more often," he told her. "What amused you so?"

"The blondes. The office was knee-deep in blondes, simply swarming all over the place. For days Chuck has been calling every model and theatrical agency in town, trying to collect blondes. Today they showed up. There must have been a hundred and fifty of them, at one time and another, every shape and size."

"And why the blondes?"

"Some promoter is trying to exploit a new section of the Florida coast. So far everything has gone wrong. First houses were put up and then wiped out by a hurricane. Then they were rebuilt and the place was struck by a tornado. Then they built a third time and a wind from the Everglades lasted five days when a big opening ceremony was planned. People were simply eaten alive by mosquitoes. So the promoter finally came to Chuck to see whether the lots could be sold from New York before the buyers got too close a look at them."

"But why the sixteen blondes?"

"They are to be photographed and paraded all over

the city on open trucks, wearing bikinis, riding surfboards, sunning themselves, swimming, playing golf—all the bait to attract the tourists. The office was a madhouse with the girls pushing and shoving, Chuck bellowing, and Julie becoming demented."

"Quite a setup for Tom."

"He seemed to be right at home. I think he loved it."

"Is that the kind of publicity stunt that so amused Brenda?"

"What amused her, I think, was that after a completely conventional life she found everything offbeat. Of course, by the time I knew her she—wasn't amused any longer. She was involved up to her chin in the Markham case."

"Involved how?"

"I don't mean that she was involved in the sense that she had anything to do with the awarding of that contract to Horace Ralston. But she knew what had happened. Anyone who watched her could tell that she was concealing something, that she was tormented."

"What did she know?"

"I don't know." As Vic's mouth twisted impatiently she added, "I really don't know." She leaned across the table. "But if it is true that someone—made her drown—"

"There's no question of it. Not any more. There was a question when I returned to New York. Then I raised the point of Brenda's murder. Within less than twenty-four hours there have been two deliberate attacks on me." Under cover of the table he raised the revolver he had taken from her handbag so she could see it. "And perhaps another scheduled for tonight?"

"That's ridiculous."

He shrugged. "While I have the revolver the point is academic. Let's get back to those alibis for the time when Brenda died. As you pointed out, I can't produce one. Neither, apparently, can you. Julie says

Ralston was with her. Mary says Markham was with her. Tom left in a dudgeon, if that's the right word. On the whole, not very satisfactory, is it?"

Before she could answer there was a sound of raised voices from the table nearest them where a man and his wife were ordering dinner.

"You don't need another cocktail," the woman said.

"Who's the best judge of that?"

"You've had three and they always make you so silly."

"You can get that way stone sober. In fact, that's your natural state."

"If you thought I was so silly, why did you beg me to marry you?"

"I must have been on the fourth drink. I can't think of any other reason."

"That's not true." The woman was beginning to whimper. "Why, you didn't even start drinking like that until after we were married."

Vic choked and looked across the table to meet Helen's eyes, which were brimming with laughter.

"Let's get out of here," she gasped.

Outside the restaurant, they leaned against the wall and shook with laughter. Finally Helen wiped her eyes. "Oh, dear," she gasped. "Oh, dear."

"The sweets of matrimony." Vic slipped his hand under her arm as they started toward the parking lot. "Careful," he warned her as he skidded on damp autumn leaves. "These things are as treacherous as ice."

She slipped, staggered wildly, her foot went out from under her, and Vic caught her, jerking her up and into his arms. He bent his head, touched her smooth cheek with his own; his lips found her mouth.

When at length he raised his head she wrenched away from him, making him stagger as his weight fell on his lame leg.

"I'm not one of your women." Her voice was shaken with rage, with what seemed almost like fear.

"Not yet." It was unforgivable and he knew it.

Her hand cracked across his face and he lost his balance. She caught his arm, steadied him, pressed the cane he had dropped into his hand. Then she walked ahead of him toward the car. He followed grimly.

But she had yielded. He could still feel the response of her lips. There was a little score to be settled. The expression on his face as he climbed into the car was not good to see.

## NINE

NEITHER OF THEM broke the silence on the twenty-minute drive to the house. Apparently Helen was familiar with the road and a competent driver. At length she went up a steep hill, turned left between big stone posts onto a circular driveway. On one side there was the long garage, equipped to accommodate four cars, with rooms above for the servants.

As the headlights moved in an arc Vic caught sight of the deep lawn behind the house, a bed of chrysanthemums, the gleam of the swimming pool, an old well, tall elms still unblighted, and an ancient oak, which held the playhouse that Bill and Brenda had been building, with a little expert but tactful help from the gardener, the year he first met them.

Then the car turned, catching the house in the headlights. It was a small Palladian structure, the narrow side facing the driveway. A short curving flagged path led from the driveway to the house. In the dark Vic was aware that there was a hedge of some kind, then lights went on over the doorway in the center of the long side of the house. Before the door opened there were running feet and a man came from the direction of the garage, pulling on a coat as he ran.

"Good evening, Ferguson," Helen said.

"Oh, it's you, Miss Manning."

"And this is Mr. Wales, the new owner."

A hard, calloused hand was thrust out. "I remember you as a kid, Mr. Wales. You used to be here a lot before you got to be so famous and went on those world tours. Always getting the twins into some kind of mischief and then I had to get them out again. It must be ten or twelve years since you was here. Glad to welcome you, I'm sure."

"Thank you," Vic said. "I'm glad that you are still around. And I'm much too old now to get anyone into mischief. I suppose the place is just the same."

"Not without the Benton twins. Not the same. And the Ellises are here now. Seem to have moved in." If a pleasant voice could be said to snarl, the caretaker snarled.

"Will you bring in the suitcases and take the car around to the garage?" Vic asked. Seeing the man's speculative look at Helen, he added quickly, "Miss Manning was good enough to drive me up. Had an accident and my leg isn't working too well."

"I heard about it. He musta been outta his head. Bill would never have done a thing like that otherwise."

Vic didn't explain that he had referred to a more recent accident. "I agree with you," he said and saw the relief on the caretaker's face. The Benton twins had made themselves loved.

The front door opened cautiously on a chain. "Who is talking out there?"

Ferguson answered. "It's Mr. Wales." He added in a tone of satisfaction, "Come home. Miss Manning drove him up."

There was a gasp and then the chain was removed and the door opened.

*Strictly poison.*

"Well," Mrs. Ellis said ungraciously, "I suppose you can come in, though we weren't expecting you. And where we can put you for the night I'm sure I don't know."

Vic had to struggle to keep his face straight as he tossed his coat and hat on a chair. The Ellises had moved in with a vengeance. Not only that, but they were prepared to defend their occupancy. He wondered whether they actually expected to bluff him into leaving.

"Anything will do," he said easily. "Tomorrow will be time enough to look around and pick out a room that suits me."

The woman stood firmly as though she half expected him to retreat. Then her mouth puckered sourly. "You're—planning to stay here then?"

Nothing was farther from Vic's thoughts, but he said in a tone of surprise, "Why, of course."

A younger woman came into the wide hallway from the long drawing room on the left.

"Bessie, this is Mr. Wales. The one who got Bill's whole estate."

"Oh." Bessie was at a loss. That, Vic suspected, was her normal state. "Well, I'm sure . . ." She held out her hand in a tentative way, rather as though she didn't know what to do with it. "We didn't expect you."

Neither of them had bothered to address Helen who looked coolly from one to the other. "I'll have my usual room, I suppose."

"Well, I guess so," Bessie said hesitantly. "Unless it's one of the rooms we are using. But no beds are made up except ours."

"I can make my own bed," Helen said. "Where are you putting Mr. Wales?"

Mrs. Ellis's eyes moved from Vic to Helen. "I guess you didn't expect anyone to be here," she said.

Hot color flooded Helen's face. Vic said, again that faint note of surprise in his voice, "Oh, Case told me that I'd find some temporary guests here." He smiled at the nonplused woman.

"I guess you can have that corner room," she said reluctantly. "I'll get out some fresh linen."

Ferguson had been standing in the doorway. Now

he came in and closed the door, setting down the suitcases. "I'll make up the beds. I always acted as houseman for Bill when he came up alone, after the house was used so little and the servants were dismissed."

"You didn't tell me that before," Mrs. Ellis snapped. "And here Bessie and I have been doing our own cooking and housework."

"I only work for the owners." Ferguson started upstairs with the suitcases.

"Well, of all things!" Mrs. Ellis turned to Vic. "What are you planning to do? Turn us out?"

"We'll discuss it in the morning." Vic's leg was hurting damnably. He walked slowly upstairs, followed by the hostile eyes of three women. He couldn't have cared less.

One side of the corner room contained a small four-poster bed, dressing table, and chest of drawers. At one end, making a sort of alcove, there was a table with an easy chair and bookshelves under the windows.

Vic eased himself into the chair and stretched out his throbbing leg with a grunt of relief. He watched in silence while Ferguson made up the bed and unpacked his bag. The caretaker was a short thickset man, with a rough thatch of gray hair and a face that was deeply lined.

"You must miss the Bentons," Vic commented.

Ferguson, on his way to the door, turned back so quickly that Vic realized he had been correct in suspecting that the man was eager to talk to him.

"That's the truth, Mr. Wales. They were nice youngsters. Known them since they were born and never met a nicer pair. That's why it seems so wicked that they should both be dead at twenty-four. They ought just to be starting. And never did a mean thing in their lives, either of 'em." He eyed Vic's leg rather belligerently as he spoke.

Vic smiled. "Bill didn't mean to do this."

"I didn't see how he could."

"And Brenda?"

"That poor kid. She come up here just the day before she died. Drowning! I would never have thought—why, she was like an eel in the water. She coulda lived in it. She—shoulda lived!"

"Just the day before she died!" Vic was startled. "How did she seem, Ferguson?"

"She looked plumb awful. Like she hadn't been sleeping. Her eyes were queer and dazed like. She looked to me like she was sick to death."

"She came just for the day?"

"No, she stayed overnight. Wandered around all over the place like she couldn't sit still."

Vic was alert. "All over the place?"

Ferguson nodded. "Looking back now, it seems almost like she had a premonition. Like it was a sort of —well, pilgrimage to all the places where she and Bill used to play." He added in a different tone, "Miss Manning come up with her."

"Why don't you like Miss Manning?"

Ferguson met his eyes directly. He seemed puzzled. "I don't just know. She's pleasant enough and she's certainly easy to look at. Not the bossy kind like the Ellises." A slow grin widened his mouth. "I guess you can deal with them. Trying to take over, that's what they've been doing. You'll have a time getting them out of here."

Vic did not seem to be disturbed. "That remains to be seen. And Miss Manning?"

"I don't know, and that's the truth. It was just— well, Brenda was acting kind of—well, as if she needed to get away by herself. And Miss Manning seemed to be following her around. Like a jailer. Meant well, I suppose." Ferguson obviously cared little for people who meant well, a point of view that had Vic's enthusiastic support. "Only it made her seem like a jailer."

Vice grinned at him. "I don't like to break down your independent stand in regard to the Ellises, but do you think you can get my breakfast in the morning?"

Ferguson returned the grin. "Sure thing. Anything else you want?"

"No, thank you. Good night, Ferguson."

II

Tired as he was, Vic had no desire to go to sleep. Long after the house was quiet, he sat almost unmoving in his chair. The Ellises, as Tom had predicted, were standing by to resist invasion. They amused him, but he was not unduly disturbed by them. They could be dealt with without trouble. What interested him was the fact that they had David Case's tacit support.

It was Brenda he found himself thinking of, Brenda who had come here looking sick to death the day before she died. Brenda who had wanted desperately to be alone. Brenda who had wandered through the house and around the grounds.

*I've left them in the usual place.*

One thing he was reasonably sure of—Brenda had not left the papers she had mentioned to Bill in the apartment. He was prepared to take his oath that he had overlooked no conceivable hiding place. Then they must be here. Q.E.D. And Helen had followed her. Like a jailer. Helen Manning.

Here Vic came to a full stop. He had had no intention of letting her become a personal problem. She wasn't his type. He tried to cling to that, but it didn't help as much as it should. Whatever she was, she stirred him profoundly. He could not be near her without having all the barriers swept away. Once before he had let himself fall in love with the wrong woman and it had proved to be disastrous. He did not intend to make the same mistake a second time.

At length he pushed himself wearily out of his chair, went to examine the revolver he had taken from her handbag. Not the usual thing a woman took on an overnight trip to a friendly house.

He felt reasonably sure now that she had engineered the attack on him the night before, that she had, with the help of her long-nosed friend, staged the attack on him earlier in the evening. And she was obviously prepared for a third incident. At least she had been until he had disarmed her. However much remained obscure, one thing became increasingly clear. Any suggestion that Brenda's death had been contrived had the instant effect of stirring up violence, and violence that was aimed at Victor Wales.

He looked for his bottle of bourbon, went in search of a bathroom, and mixed a drink. There was no ice, but he wasn't going to hunt through a house whose layout he had almost forgotten. He came back to his room, switched out the lights, and turned his chair so that he could look from the window. There was a full moon. His room was high enough so that he could see over the hedge the circular line of the driveway, the dark structure of the garage.

He sipped his drink, wondered vaguely whether Tom was already drunk, thought of Mary toppling over when he said that Brenda had been murdered. Mary and her hatred of Brenda. Mary and the man Markham crying out to her that he couldn't take any more.

Vic ran his fingers through his hair. There were too many unanswered questions, and the problem was that he did not yet know which ones were relevant.

Absently he ran the fingers of his left hand over the back of the right, felt the welt, was aware of the tide of bitterness and despair that he had hoped was fading away. Would he never recover from this? The fingers continued to probe the crippled hand. What had the doctor told him at the time? With therapy and infinite patience he could restore function. But it might take years and he had no years to waste. By the time his hand was restored it would be too late to regain his technique. And he was damned if he was going to follow the example, heroic, no doubt, of pianists with amputated or crippled right hands who devoted their energies to doing music for the left hand alone. He'd play or he'd quit. But no halfway measures.

What had Helen said about his recording of the Schumann Fantasia? Forget it!

He closed his eyes as though shutting out the intolerable, opened them again. Blinked. There had been a brief flash of light on the lawn at the back of the house. Nonsense, it was the moonlight reflected on something.

He got out of his chair and went to stand at the window. There was no light. Then as his eyes adjusted he began to see the dark shape of the elms, the gleam of the pool, still unemptied, though it was unlikely anyone had used it in months, unless Brenda—he shut that thought away too.

There was some dark object on the lawn. He frowned, staring hard. Then he remembered. That was the old well, which the Bentons had refused to remove though it had been unused for a couple of generations. Beside it something stirred. Again there was a quick flash of light. Someone was peering into the well.

Vic reached for Helen's revolver, slipped it in his pocket, picked up his cane, opened the door, and groped his way down the stairs, holding the banister to guide him. Behind the closed bedroom doors nothing moved. Whoever was investigating the old well was unlikely to be a member of the household. There would be better and far safer opportunities by daylight.

In the hallway he stumbled over a chair, which seemed to make an enormous racket. He rubbed his knee, cursing softly to himself, and then listened. Apparently the noise had disturbed no one. He had to fumble with the chain on the door before he could remove it, then found a bolt. At last the door opened.

When he found himself in front of the house he cursed again softly. He wasn't using his head. Now he would have to go all around, and heaven only knew what obstacles there were in the form of hedges, flower beds, and trees to interfere. Still he would probably have been no better off going through the house because he had forgotten the layout, forgotten even where the doors were that led to the back lawn.

He made the easier choice by following the flagged path, dimly discernible by moonlight, to the driveway, turned left, passed the kitchen door, was suddenly on the lawn. Now he could see the well, see the dark figure crouching over it. But he was visible too. There was a strangled gasp and then the dark figure was straightening up. Vic braced himself, gripped the weighted cane, lunged forward. The other moved fast, racing past the well, toward the other side of the house.

There was no chance of catching him, so Vic turned back to cut him off when he appeared in front.

He waited in the shadow of a hedge, watching the dark side of the house, but aware, too, of the curving driveway on the other side. Three minutes passed. He knew then that the man had eluded him. But where the hell could he have gone?

He whirled around as someone ran across the driveway and then he saw that it was Ferguson.

"What's going on?"

"We've got a prowler looking at the well."

"The well!"

Vic explained what had happened. "I don't know how he managed to get away."

"He must have come through the house. There are French doors at the end of the long drawing room and a door onto the terrace from the small living room." Ferguson looked at the cane. "Don't try to run. You stay here to cut him off." He turned back into the house.

Vic waited in an agony of frustration, leaning

heavily on his cane. Then he turned to the left, unable to bear the inaction, and started to make his way around the house. As he reached the corner, Ferguson leaped at him and then swore.

"Mr. Wales! Why didn't you stay where I told you?" He ran back, opened the door of the long drawing room. A moment later he returned.

"He escaped through the house as soon as you were out of the way." Panting, he ran toward the driveway. That, Vic recalled, was the only possible approach to the house, the only escape from it, as it was shut off from the road by a thick and practically impenetrable hedge. Certainly impenetrable in the dark.

When Ferguson came back at last he was scowling. "I can't figure how he slipped out. There's not a sign of him on the road, and no car drove away from here."

"Unless," Vic said slowly, "our intruder hasn't left the house at all."

Together the two men went through the ground floor, room by room. A huge drawing room ran the width of the house on the left side, with French doors opening on the lawn. A wide entrance hall extended from the drawing room on the left to the big formal dining room on the right. In between there was a small living room and a ground-floor bedroom with bath because the older Benton had had a heart condition and could not climb stairs. Beyond was the staircase, a powder room, and past the dining room a smaller breakfast room, pantries, kitchen, laundry and drying rooms, and the sitting room, with its radio and television, for the servants who no longer worked there.

Together the two men climbed to the second floor, switching on lights. There were six bedrooms, two of which shared a hall bathroom; the others had their own baths. From behind Nora Ellis's door came the sound of her heavy snoring. Bessie was awake and stirring. From behind her closed door she whispered in an agitated way, "Who is it? What's going on?"

"Ferguson, ma'am, and Mr. Wales. We're just checking up. Thought there was a prowler."

Bessie gave a frightened squeal and opened her door a trifle. She wore pajamas; her hair was on end, and she was half asleep and half demented.

"It's happened several times, we told you that. We've heard someone around the place, but you wouldn't pay any attention. We'll be killed in our beds."

This idea did not appear to distress Ferguson. He tapped on Helen's door. After a brief interval she opened it. Unlike Bessie, she did not inquire first who was there. She wore a wool robe, but as she turned swiftly Vic could see that under it she had black velvet slacks and a dark sweater. She was breathing quickly, but with haste rather than alarm.

She looked at Vic and lied blandly. She had seen and heard nothing. She had been sound asleep when he knocked on the door.

When Ferguson had returned to his rooms over the garage, Vic finally went to bed. For a long time he sweated out the pain in his leg. Then as it subsided he tried to sleep, but he was wide awake. Was it Helen Manning or someone else who had been examining the well? He must be sure to search it in the morning.

Who had been hunting for the papers Brenda had left behind her? What a hornet's nest she had stirred up! Sick to death, Ferguson had said. Like Bill. He remembered the expression of horror that had faded from Bill's face when he died while Vic was removing the letter from his wallet. As though he knew. Had Brenda known too? He hoped she hadn't.

# TEN

SHORTLY BEFORE six o'clock Ferguson opened Vic's door quietly and came in with a cup of coffee. While Vic drank it the two men talked in low tones. It was true, Ferguson said, that the Ellises had complained several times about someone prowling around the grounds, that they insisted attempts had been made to break into the house.

Okay, he went on defensively, though Vic made no criticism, he should have done something about it, as his only real job any more was that of watchman, but, in the first place, he hadn't believed them, a couple of silly women; in the second place, the way they had tried to take over the Benton house had burned him and he had no intention of lifting a hand for them. They had even threatened to rent his apartment over the garage for the additional income, until they found out that Bill had left it to him for his lifetime. That had really set them off, particularly the old lady. Bill had done something for everyone but his own family, and it had a queer look. A very queer look. She'd get to the bottom of it if that was the last thing she did.

Seeing his new employer's relaxed amusement, Ferguson grinned. The truth was that neither of the twins had ever liked the Ellises. All that restrained them as youngsters was having their parents lay down the law. When they were older their natural good manners had carried the situation so the Ellises hadn't guessed how they felt. And then, the caretaker ruminated, some people never see anything they don't want to see.

"Well," he said at last, when Vic had finished his coffee and begun to dress, "we'll take a look at the well before—anyone is up and around. Spying."

"You think so, too, then."

"Miss Manning? What else can we think? No one got away from the house—I sat at my window for two hours watching the driveway—and you saw what she had on under that robe she was wearing. And out of breath. Only what she was looking for in the old well is more than I can figure out."

After they had examined the well with a big flashlight and Ferguson had climbed cautiously down the heavy rope, it was still more than either man could figure out.

"I'll take my oath there's nothing down there. So why would anyone . . ." Ferguson began when the two men had abandoned the search and gone to the kitchen where Ferguson cooked breakfast.

"Did the Benton twins ever have a favorite hiding place as kids?" Vic asked.

Ferguson turned around from the stove with a slow grin. "Always up to tricks those kids were. And you put them up to about half of them. But hiding place? I don't know. They were so—well, a part of each other, you know, that they didn't confide much in anyone else. Used to be they spent half their time in that playhouse up in the oak tree. I can remember once . . ."

She came in without a sound. It was the whiff of light perfume that alerted them.

Vic got to his feet. "Good morning, Miss Manning. You're up early."

"I am a wage earner. I must get back to New York this morning. Ferguson, do you have a time table?"

"You can drive me back," Vic suggested.

"But you intended to stay on, didn't you?"

"I hadn't made any plans." Vic raised his brows at Ferguson who shrugged and set about preparing more eggs, bacon, and toast.

As soon as they had finished eating he cleared up with alacrity. "I'm not cooking for the Ellises. What are you going to do about them, Mr. Wales?"

Vic shrugged. "We'll let it ride for the time being." Seeing the caretaker's expression, he added reassuringly, "Don't worry, I'll clear them out permanently when the time comes."

The drive back to New York was a silent one. Helen Manning made no reference to last night's disturbance, which rather amused him. They had passed Yonkers before he reached for her handbag and put the revolver in it. Even then she had nothing to say, though he thought he saw the corner of her mouth turn up for a moment.

She stopped the car before the Beekman House apartment. "I'll pick up a cab here," she said, and she was gone before he could speak.

Winnie, who had been making Tom's bed, came into the hallway when Vic opened the door of the apartment. Mr. Keith, she reported, had gone to work. There were some calls for Mr. Wales, one from Miss Mary Smith, one from Mr. Fedder, and a third from a gentleman who had refused to leave his name.

It was too early to call Mary who rarely got up before noon. Chuck Fedder had apparently been waiting for the call. He wanted to see Vic. It was important, but he couldn't talk now, the office was bedlam; anyhow, what he had to say was private.

It might be better if Vic didn't come to the office. Or, Chuck added after a slight pause, to the apartment. There were too many people to listen in. Too many people who . . . Another pause.

"How about my apartment this evening?" Vic suggested.

"Uh—well, maybe a bar somewhere would be better. You're on the wrong track, you know, but maybe if we put our heads together—" Chuck broke off and said sharply, "Damn it, Julie, can't I make a single telephone call in peace? I don't care who it is." He spoke into the telephone again. "Well, I'll be seeing you. I'll be in touch." And the connection was broken.

So Chuck didn't want Julie to know he was talking to Victor Wales, that he was planning to meet him. And he thought Vic was on the wrong track.

Before he could telephone Mary she called him. "Vic, we didn't really talk when you came yesterday. And then—and—we can't talk really until after the opening tomorrow night. I haven't a free moment. Honestly. Oh, I'm sending you tickets. And I'm having some people in later to wait for the reviews. Just a small party. You'll come, of course. And bring your woman."

"What woman?"

"How should I know? Then we'll arrange to have a—long talk. Uninterrupted. Please, Vic."

"Of course."

After a moment's hesitation he phoned the Fedder office again and this time got Helen Manning, who sounded businesslike and crisp. Somewhat to his surprise she accepted promptly. She'd be delighted to see the opening of *Forever and Yesterday* with him. She didn't, Vic thought, sound delighted.

As the afternoon advanced, he was increasingly restless. He should have stayed at the Connecticut house until he found Brenda's papers. Returning to New York for the sake of making the trip with Helen had been an act of stupidity. One way or another he would have to break the hold she had on him because he could not afford to make mistakes.

He had smoked half a dozen cigarettes in rapid succession when the door chimes sounded and he found himself face to face with John Markham. He stepped silently aside to let the man enter, waved his visitor to a chair, which he accepted, and offered him a cigarette, which he refused. Then he waited.

"I think it's time that we clear the decks," Markham said at last. "More than time. I should have done this in the beginning, but Mary talked me out of it." He looked at Vic and smiled. For the first time Vic was aware of the man's great charm, which was not a matter of surface tricks but a revelation of his real personality. "A poor excuse, I agree," he went on as though Vic had spoken. "Hiding behind a woman's skirts. And that's pretty much what I've been doing for the past six months."

"It seems to me," Vic said mildly, "that you've come to the wrong place with this confession. Shouldn't you be making it in Washington?"

Markham looked at him blankly. Then his face cleared. "Good God! I haven't come to confess that I took that bribe. I never saw the money. I never heard of the Ralston contract until rumors began floating around about me. Never. It's as much a mystery to me as it is to everyone else. No, if I could clear that filthy mess, I'd be shouting from the housetops. And I believe I could kill the person who did that to me." He didn't emphasize his words, but Vic believed him.

He lighted a cigarette and waited. Markham said unexpectedly, "You're a cold-blooded devil!"

Vic shrugged. "So far there's been no occasion for me to break down and cry."

Markham's hand tightened on the arm of his chair. "What brought me here," he said, "was the unholy mess that has developed because"—he laughed quietly—"because, God forgive me, I meant well. And I've ended by messing up the lives of three women."

The cigarette burned Vic's fingers before he remembered to put it out. "If you've come here to astonish me," he said at last, "you have succeeded. But what you think I can do—"

"Wait, please." There was nothing peremptory in Markham's slight gesture, but it carried authority. "All this is as embarrassing as hell because I haven't made a practice of discussing my private life with strangers. But after seeing what you did to Mary yesterday, I knew this thing had to end. After all, you're an old friend of hers. You've loved her enough at one time to be willing to hurt her now. And you are a friend of her husband. One of his oldest and best friends."

Vic watched him steadily, but he did not attempt to help him out.

"The thing is," Markham said, "in spite of your insinuation that Mary was unfaithful, she has never loved anyone in her life but her husband. I am not her lover. I never was. I never aspired to be. If Keith had had the brains of a ten-year-old, he would have known that for himself. As I figure him out, he's jealous not merely of other men but of Mary's tremendous success, of the fact that her income is easily ten times as large as his."

Vic got up to ease his leg and stood at the window, his back to his uninvited guest.

"Did you ever hear of Norma Wellington?" Markham asked abruptly.

Vic turned around in surprise and shook his head.

"Ten years ago she was just getting a start, a minor actress with walk-on parts. Only eighteen and the prettiest thing I ever saw. I married her." Seeing Vic's astonishment, he said, "It was never made public, but it was no secret either. Of course, I wasn't a public figure then. We had only been married a year when I discovered Norma was a drug addict. I did everything I could to help her. I think she tried too. Doctors. Hospitals. Cures. She'd come home and I'd watch her and then, sooner or later, she would get hold of the stuff again. Once she was picked up for shoplifting to get money. That time she used her stage name to protect me. Whatever we had she sold so she could buy the stuff. Kept me strapped all the time. Which, if the papers had only known it, would have provided a sure-fire motive for taking that bribe.

"Well, the President began to use me as a special adviser, sent me abroad on diplomatic missions, that sort of thing. I began to get a lot of publicity of one sort and another. Norma—she's still in love with me, as I am with her—wanted to go away, get a quiet divorce, make a clear break for my sake.

"It was Mary, who had known her long before

we were married, who came up with the suggestion that we try once more. She has a Connecticut house, though she is rarely there. She planned to take Norma there with an attendant who would be part nurse and part—bodyguard, I guess. And, with that magnificent loyalty of hers, she didn't even tell Keith.

"We took Norma up there and she began to get better. She was less nervous; she put on weight. She did a bit of swimming and sun bathing on the beach. Whenever I could I went up to visit her. I don't believe Mary and I ever happened to be there at the same time except once when she came up unexpectedly to get some clothes she had left at the house. Keith had been in Chicago doing some advance publicity and that night he came back and turned up unexpectedly.

"As luck would have it, Norma had been in a difficult state all day. One of the weeklies published a long article about me and she thought she was ruining my life. She was hysterical, and both Mary and I were trying to reason with her, calm her down. It must have been about three in the morning; we'd both been awakened by Norma crying, and we wearing pajamas and robes.

"When the car drove up, her attendant got Norma away and gave her a sedative. Tom came in and found me with Mary. He was like a madman. The things he said to her . . ."

Markham broke off, his hand shaking. Mary, he went on, had stood like a woman turned to stone. That marriage—but everyone knew what the marriage had seemed to be, built on a rock. And she made no defense. She refused to allow Markham to make any defense. It wasn't Norma she was protecting at this point. She had taken for granted Tom's absolute faith in her. It was that faith she wanted now. Even when he turned and flung out of the house she said nothing.

Tom Keith had not gone back to their New York

apartment for days. When he did so he was drunk and offensive.

"I wanted to tell him the truth," Markham said, "but Mary wouldn't let me. She said this was her problem, hers and Tom's. What mattered was not that she should be proved innocent; it was that Tom should believe her to be innocent. If he couldn't do that, then nothing they had built between them had any meaning at all.

"So I let the thing ride, even when Mary finally told Tom not to come back until he believed in her, until he could come without questions and without doubts. But now, after hearing your snide comments, I know I was wrong. Anyone who told you that Mary was two-timing Tom deserved to have his neck wrung. That's about all." Markham started to get up.

Vic spoke for the first time. "You said—three women."

Markham sank back in his chair. "Oh yes, of course. I had almost forgotten. Brenda Benton."

"Everyone seems to forget the Bentons."

"Brenda wasn't a very—memorable person."

"Brenda who understands," Vic quoted softly.

Markham looked at him, brows furrowed. "Oh, you found my book. That inscription, however, was a mistake. Brenda didn't understand. I think she believed, as Keith did, that I was Mary's lover."

"And even believing that, she practically went to the stake for you?"

"No," Markham said definitely, "not for me. She was—I don't know how well you knew her—"

"I've known her since she was ten."

Markham swept that away. "It doesn't matter what you knew of her at ten. At twenty-four she was —fuzzy-minded, loyal, romantic. And I am not the man she was in love with, Wales. No man can mistake a situation like that. I never, God knows, made a play for her. Since I first met Norma I've never wanted another woman. No, I think Brenda fell in love with Ralston. He's an older man with the kind of assurance both the Bentons completely lacked."

Odd, Vic thought, he had never realized that for himself.

"For Brenda he must have had glamour. That he made a deal to get that contract I've never doubted for a moment. And I think Brenda covered for him the only way she knew how, by keeping still."

"And where was Ralston when she died?" Vic asked.

"I spent last night trying to remember everything about that birthday party. The truth is that I'd come out to see Norma. When Ralston put in an appearance I was furious, of course, but I thought it was a trick of the Fedders. Mary got me away on some pretext, and then I went up to see Norma. It was while I was with my wife that poor Brenda went in swimming. I had started back to New York before they began to be worried about her. And that's all I know about the whole situation. The reason I came to you with this is because Mary has been a wonderful friend. I couldn't sit back and let you attack her again as you did yesterday."

Markham got to his feet, took a long look at Vic, and then let himself out of the apartment. For a long time after he had gone Vic moved restlessly around the room. At length he gave up and went out, hailed a cab, and drove to the building that housed the offices of Chuck Fedder. The time was four forty-five.

In the lobby he bought a package of cigarettes and then he drifted out onto the street again. But what he was waiting for he was hanged if he knew. He had come because he had to come. It was as simple, as irrational, as that. Or perhaps not irrational. The key to unlock the mystery of the Markham affair and Brenda's death lay somewhere in the Fedder office.

At the end of five minutes the door revolved, discharging people onto the sidewalk. One of them was a tall, lush blonde wearing a mink coat. The weather was far too mild for it and the coat swung wide open. Vic would have stepped forward if Julie Fedder's manner had not been so odd. For a moment she stood against the side of the building waiting, but no one else came through the revolving door. Then she turned and scuttled along the street, as though shrinking against the side of the building, to a small doorway. Over the door was the sign, "Quilp's Cocktail Lounge." She darted inside.

For ten minutes Vic waited, but no one appeared to be following Julie, so at last he went in. On the right there was a curving bar, on the left small tables; at the back there were booths. The place was as nearly dark as was possible and still make it practicable for waiters to move back and forth.

When his eyes had become adjusted to the gloom, Vic looked at the tables and then strolled toward the back. Julie was in the second booth, and the man with whom she was talking was Horace Ralston. Vic went past and found that the third booth was empty.

A waiter who appeared to have the eyesight of an owl took his order and returned in a short time with bourbon and water and a small dish of salted nuts.

For a time he could make out only a murmur from the booth behind him. Then he began to distinguish words. The voice was Julie's. Whatever this was, it did not appear to be the meeting of lovers. It sounded more like the acrimonious argument of a married couple.

". . . just listen to me. That's all I ask."

"That will be the day," Ralston commented.

"Oh, shut up! Just shut up! I'll tell you one thing, I know men."

"You ought to."

"He won't give up. The whole thing is going to come out."

"Changed your tune, haven't you?"

"The story line has changed too. With Brenda's murder—"

Vic set his glass noiselessly on the table. If only his ears had antennae! He held his breath.

"So it's murder now," Ralston said softly, and something even in that suppressed voice made the hair stand up on the back of Vic's neck.

"You think you can bully your way through anything," Julie muttered.

"Well?"

"Well, I tell you the whole business has gone up in smoke. We're sitting on the edge of a volcano and I can hear it rumble."

"Wales seems to have you hypnotized."

"It's more than Wales. Chuck has the wind up. He is planning something. I can sense it; I know him so well. But he won't tell me. And like a fool he hired Tom Keith. That boy's maybe turning into an alcoholic, and that makes him unpredictable. We don't want him there. He . . . Horace, what with one thing and another I'm scared to death."

"You had better be," Ralston said. "You hear me?" Julie gave a stifled scream. "Quiet! You hear me?"

"I hear you," she said sullenly.

"Then listen to this. You had better watch your step. I don't fool."

"Maybe you think you can scare Wales to death too. I'll tell you one thing. That guy doesn't scare."

Ralston gave a stifled laugh. "One way or another, Wales will be taken care of."

"What are you going to do?"

"I didn't say I was going to do anything." A tone of elaborate surprise. Then, "What's his connection with Helen Manning?"

"I—why, he never met her until he came back to New York."

"Then she's a fast worker."

"You're telling me. It didn't take you long to shift to Helen, did it? It didn't take—"

"Cut it out! Use your head for once, if you know how. Helen is making a big play for Wales. Is that because of the Benton money or—"

"What else?"

"That's what I want to know. Get smart and find out." Ralston stood up. "I have an appointment. You ready to go?"

"I'll have another drink," Julie said.

"Suit yourself." Ralston moved out of the booth. Vic heard his heavy, assured tread down the length of the bar. Then there was a rustle of sound and Julie stood beside his booth. For a long moment they examined each other in slience.

"May I buy you a drink?" he asked.

"Why not?" Julie said.

When the waiter had taken their orders she leaned across the table. "Mr. Wales, how much would you be willing to pay to know the truth about the Markham case?"

# ELEVEN

BESIDE HIM IN the darkened theater Helen stirred, and Vic was acutely aware of her. Why did this have to happen? She wasn't his type. He wouldn't trust her out of sight. She was cold and calculating and she had nerves of steel. He had always liked yielding women, helpless women. But no woman had ever so stirred his senses. He was angry with her, angry with himself, and completely helpless.

On the stage Mary Smith worked her usual miracle. An infatuated audience responded to her smiles, to her husky voice, to her infectious gaiety. Like most musicals this one had little plot and what there was made little sense. But it didn't matter.

While Mary was on the stage there was excitement and delight.

During the intermission, while Vic and Helen were having a cigarette in the lobby, Helen touched his arm. John Markham was standing near them, an unlighted cigarette in his hand. Though he must be aware of the curious eyes, the whispers and nudges as people recognized him, his face remained impassive, his eyes abstracted, deliberately avoiding the necessity of speech.

There was a little stir as Tom Keith pushed his way roughly through a group of people and came face to face with Markham. Tom, as Vic had noticed before he left the apartment earlier in the evening, was drunk.

Helen's hand tightened on Vic's arm. "You've got to break it up," she said in a low tone. "Do something. Hurry!" She gave him a little push.

Tom leaned forward, swaying, until his face was not a foot away from the other man's. "You crooked bastard!"

Vic moved then, seized Tom's arm, pulled him away, and at the same time he looked at Markham, jerking his head toward the door. Markham, his face very white, turned and made his way back into the theater.

"You damned fool!" Vic growled.

Tom stood swaying and grinning at him, with something boyish in his smile. "I've wanted to do that for a long, long time." Even with his mouth slack from drinking he retained much of his good looks.

"So you've had your fun."

"You're wrong," Tom said with a delighted smile. "I'm just leading up to it."

"Let it drop, Tom, for God's sake!"

Tom laughed. "Spoilsport."

Vic shook the arm he held. "Listen to me." He kept his voice low, conscious of the malicious eyes that watched them both. The audience tonight was getting two shows for the price of one. "Don't make a scene now. Not tonight. This is Mary's night. You know actresses can't afford this sort of publicity."

"Mary." Tom's voice broke on his wife's name. He tried to free himself. "I should have killed him while I was about it."

"So help me," Vic said savagely, "if you don't quiet down, I'll drag you away from here and knock you out."

"You're still in love with her, aren't you? Bill knew that. Why didn't I see it?" With a jerk Tom freed his arm. "I might have known the Great Lover wouldn't let anyone like Mary get away." The movement threw him momentarily off balance. Then he thrust his way through the crowd and went out onto the street.

The buzzer sounded its warning and Vic found Helen close beside him. In silence they returned to their seats as the house lights dimmed.

Once during the second act he was roused by a roar of laughter from the audience and he looked up to find Helen watching him curiously. He wondered in some discomfort what she had been reading in his face. Then he forgot her again.

At last there was a storm of applause, the usual confusion as seats were pushed back and people stood, put on coats, talked and laughed and still applauded. The curtains swept aside and the cast was lined up, then the featured performers bowed alone, and finally Mary appeared by herself. There were shouts and cheers. Standing with her arms widespread, as though embracing them all, the big heartwarming smile on her lips, she looked very small.

Then the house lights went up, the orchestra reprised the hit song, and the audience jammed the aisles. Vic slipped Helen's evening coat over her bare shoulders, careful not to touch her. They remained seated.

"There will be a mob backstage," he said. "No

point in getting into it. We may as well let the crowd get out and then we can go to Sardi's for a drink. That will give Mary time to greet all her admirers backstage, change, and go home."

"Sardi's will be crowded, too," Helen pointed out.

"I reserved a table."

"You think of everything, don't you?"

"If I had, I'd have slugged Tom before I left him this evening. It never occurred to me that he would turn up here and try to pull something like that. The one thing I thought he was incapable of was making a public display about Mary."

"She was marvelous, wasn't she?" Helen commented after a long silence.

"Terrific. But she always is. And she has that special quality that distinguishes the great ones from all the runners-up."

"What's that?" Vic thought her expression was rather odd, but so was her whole attitude in regard to Mary.

"She's herself. Mary Smith. Like no one else in the world."

"I wonder what she would have thought if she had known about that scene her husband made in the lobby."

"I don't know what she would have thought, but the show would have gone on just the same."

"What broke them up? His drinking?" When he made no reply she said, "It seems queer. Markham, of course, is the more impressive man, but certainly Tom Keith is the more attractive."

"You think so?"

"Any woman would think so." Helen added rather tartly, "Except his wife."

II

By the time Vic and Helen reached Mary's apartment the party was already going strong. As Vic had anticipated, Mary's "little" party jammed the rooms to the doors. The chief members of the cast, the producer, director, backers were all present and all exuberant. It was unnecessary to wait for the reviews. They knew they had a smash hit.

Mary was like a flame. She kissed Vic and held out her hand to Helen, though her face stiffened when she recognized her. "How nice of Vic to bring you," she murmured. Helen's, "You were marvelous, Miss Smith," was so tepid that Vic smothered a grin. The two young women eyed each other like Japanese wrestlers before the fray. Then his grin faded. It would be interesting to know what had sparked this naked hostility.

Standing apart from the group, staring out at the dark expanse of Central Park and the lights of Fifth Avenue and Central Park West, was John Markham, holding an untouched highball glass. What had brought him here, Vic wondered. From every standpoint his presence in Mary's apartment was a mistake. It justified Tom's jealousy; it confirmed the gossip that floated through the press about them.

During that curious monologue in Vic's apartment, Markham had convinced him of his sincerity. He had believed that his love for the wayward Norma Wellington was genuine, that his interest in Mary was that only of grateful friendship. Now it appeared that the man who showed so much insight into the motives of others was blind to his own condition. His tortured cry when he had entered Mary's apartment, "Mary, I've got to see you. I can't take any more," was the expression of a man who had become emotionally dependent upon a woman.

Waiters were circulating with trays of drinks and Vic captured two glasses, handed one to Helen, and was about to speak when, above the talk and the laughter, there were raised voices. Mary turned sharply toward the door, her eyes wide with shock.

Tom appeared, herding before him the Fedders

and Horace Ralston. His three guests were resplendent in evening clothes, but Tom, as Vic had seen him in the lobby, was untidy in a rumpled business suit, his hair mussed. He went straight to Mary, put his arms around her, and kissed her on the mouth. When he looked up his eyes were bright.

"I came to help celebrate your great success." He enunciated slowly and with great care. "Haven't seen it myself. Too drunk. But it's sure to be a success. Mary Smith is always a success."

He made a wide gesture that knocked the glass out of the hand of a man standing near him. "Brought some friends." He waved to the three people who hovered in the doorway to come forward. "You know the Fedders. Great friends of mine, the Fedders. Took me on, gave me a job, after you fired me. No more board. No more bed. And Horace Ralston. Great friend too. Friend of a friend, if you know what I mean. Friend of your friend. Where's Markham? Where's the great presidential adviser? Don't tell me Markham isn't here. You can't have a party without the presidential adviser. They say he's out of a job too."

Mary stood motionless, so white under the makeup that Vic thought she was going to faint. Oddly enough, it was Julie Fedder who broke the stricken silence that held everyone paralyzed with embarrassment.

"Sorry, Mary. This was Tom's idea. I thought it was just a gag so he could get to see you. Right here and now I'm finished. Nobody hooks me into another mess. That's final." She took Ralston's arm. "Come on, Horace. Tom's drunk. We don't want to get mixed up in a fight. There's been enough scandal."

"You giving me orders?" Ralston asked softly.

"Just a warning." She waved at Vic. "Be seeing you," she said defiantly.

Chuck Fedder seized his wife's wrist. "You aren't going anywhere except with me. Is that clear?"

His wife stared at him, heard the menace in his voice, and released Ralston's arm, trying to laugh.

Ralston bowed to Mary. "You were wonderful tonight, Miss Smith. Absolutely wonderful. And I'm sorry if we've caused you any embarrassment." He caught sight of Vic, hesitated, and then came up to him. He would, Vic thought, have liked to strangle Julie Fedder for her share in the embarrassing scene, and he was annoyed because Vic had witnessed it.

"We meet again, Mr. Wales. I'd forgotten you were such a good friend of Miss Smith's."

Vic grinned at him. "Too old a friend to have to crash the party."

Ralston, Vic saw with satisfaction, didn't like that at all. "Seem to have got our signals mixed," he said lightly.

"At least the warning signal is clear," Vic told him.

Ralston turned abruptly, and brushed past the Fedders without a word or a look, and went out of the room.

Chuck's thick hand tightened on his wife's wrist. "We're going home."

Vic reached them before they could leave. "Take Tom with you."

"Why should we?" Julie protested. "I've had it right up to here."

Chuck looked at Vic and said hastily, "Okay, we'll take him if you can get him out."

"I'll get him out." Vic went back to Tom who stood smiling at Mary, weaving on his feet. "You've had your fun. Get on your horse."

The smile faded from Tom's face. He looked at his wife, his eyes dark with pain. "I'm sorry. Oh God, I'm sorry." He obeyed the pressure of Vic's hand and went out with the Fedders.

A few minutes later, after giving them a safe margin of time in which to find a taxi, Markham made an unobtrusive departure.

Everyone did his valiant best, but the party had

died on its feet. At length Mary got up on a stool and held out her arms.

"It's no use, is it? Things have gone wrong. Perhaps you would all—please—"

With mumbled comments they drifted awkwardly away in small groups.

"Well," Helen said on a long breath when the doorman had put them in a taxi.

"Is it?" Vic asked somberly.

"Why did Keith do a thing like that? Such an unforgivable thing? And bringing those people with him! He's so terribly in love with his wife. Why did he want to hurt her?"

"I suppose that was why." Vic remembered Markham telling him that afternoon that he had hurt Mary because he loved her.

"I thought Horace Ralston, at least, had more sense and better manners than to consent to barge in on a party that way. He certainly must have known that Miss Smith wouldn't want him. After all, everyone knows how she feels about Markham."

"Do they?"

Helen turned to look at him. "You must know what people say about them."

"What people say!" Vic laughed shortly.

Helen smoothed the long white kid gloves. It seemed to her that the man at her side had withdrawn beyond reach. When he spoke she realized that his thoughts had drifted away from the course her own were following.

"I'd like to know what prompted the Fedders to go there tonight."

"Well," Helen said slowly, "there were bound to be a lot of celebrities, and people on the fringes who could do with a public-relations outfit. And that's the way they have worked for years. Not crashing parties, but using parties as a means of introducing people, bringing them together . . ."

"Making contacts," Vic said.

"I know. I hate the phrase too. But that's the

method that has helped them pull off a lot of deals. The third drink and a little flattery and meeting the right people and the right suggestion at the right time—you know how it works."

"And that's the way the Ralston contract was managed?"

Helen shrugged and withdrew into her corner of the cab.

"Julie Fedder really is a fool!" Vic exclaimed. "That woman is asking for trouble, and I think she is quite likely to get it."

"From her husband, you mean, or from Horace Ralston?"

"You'd know more about that than I do." Vic got out and helped her from the cab. "Good night and thank you for coming."

"Would you mind walking to the door with me? The garden is so dark and—somehow I'm nervous tonight. Too much has happened."

"Of course." They walked in silence through the apartment hallway and the dark garden. At her door Helen fumbled in her evening bag for the key, turned it in the lock, and gasped.

"I put the lights out when I left the house. I'm positive I did."

Vic took a long look at her, but she seemed genuinely unnerved, unaware of him. Had the whole excursion to her house been the oldest trick in the world? Was it trick or treat?

Stepping ahead of her, Vic went into the big studio room while she remained at the door. Everything seemed to be in order. No sign of an intruder. Then he saw that someone was lying on the huge couch before the fireplace. Vic approached quietly, gripping his cane.

"Well, I'm damned!"

"Who is it?" Helen asked, a quaver in her voice.

"Tom Keith. Out like a light."

"Tom!" She came forward, her face incredulous,

looked down at the recumbent figure. "How did he get in here?" She seemed genuinely bewildered.

"Did you ever give him a key?"

He was surprised to see her face flame. "Of course not. What can we do with him? I don't want him here."

"In his condition he's harmless enough. I don't think anything short of an earthquake would rouse him."

"Just the same I don't want him to stay."

Vic looked thoughtfully at Tom. Then he shrugged. "Okay, lady. Always happy to oblige." He bent over, hoisted Tom onto his shoulder, and started for the door, hoping his leg would hold up under the strain. The taxi driver, long past the day of surprises, got out to help him with the unconscious man. Vic sat with Tom's head on his shoulder, fumes of alcohol breathed into his face.

When the doorman at the Beekman Place apartment came to help him with Tom, Vic surprised him by saying explosively, "Julie!"


## TWELVE

THE ELEVATOR MAN eased Tom onto his bed and shook his head. "Man, is he loaded! He must have had a gallon. Never saw him pass out before." Dexterously he palmed the bill Vic gave him and went out.

Vic stood staring down at Tom, saw an eyebrow twitch. He hoped Tom wasn't going to wake up. Not tonight. He looked at his watch. Two-thirty. What was left of the night? He'd been a fool to carry the man. He grinned to himself. Served him right. Showing off his manly strength like a teenager to impress Helen, who hadn't seemed to be impressed.

Tom lay without moving. The easiest way out,

Vic thought bitterly. A pity he hadn't got that drunk before he set out on his evening's capers. From that gratuitously nasty little scene in the theater lobby to his eruption into Mary's party he had done his best to end any hope of a reconciliation with his wife.

The pursuit of happiness! Who had stated that man's chief drive was the pursuit of happiness? Anyone who used his eyes knew better. Men were more apt to seek their own destruction. *Mine own executioner.* That was more like it.

And while he was in this philosophic mood, Vic reminded himself sardonically, he might take a detached look at the case of Victor Wales. The trouble was that it was easy to criticize others; somehow he found himself trying to justify Wales. Irritably he reached out to switch off the light burning down on Tom's defenseless face.

He limped into his own room and sagged on the side of the bed, bending over to rub his leg. His eyes caught a faint movement. The closet door was opening stealthily, a slow inch at a time. He gripped his cane and stood up. For a moment he feared that his leg was going to buckle under him; the pain brought out a cold sweat. Nevertheless, as the door opened, he moved step by step so that it concealed him.

The two men, stockings tied over the lower part of their faces, came out with a rush. Vic swung his cane, catching one of them across the kneecap. He let out a howl of pain and staggered, but the second man kept coming. Vic lurched forward, his weight on the lame leg, and fell, the goon on top of him. Hands reached for his throat; fingers dug in. He brought up his knee and the other man rolled away, moaning. Vic scrambled to his feet.

The first man had recovered his balance and swung at him, his fist catching him in the pit of the stomach. As he fell his weight overturned the bedside table. The telephone crashed on the floor, a vase shattered beside it.

"May I help you?" came the tinny voice of the man at the downstairs switchboard.

"Help!" Vic shouted. "Help! Police!"

The two men jostled each other as they made for the door. A moment later the outside door closed. Vic tried to pull himself to his feet and found that they would not take his weight. He heard the two-toned chimes and then a key turned in the lock.

"Mr. Wales?"

"Here."

The doorman came in, accompanied by a uniformed policeman. Together they got Vic onto the side of the bed.

"Patrol car just passing," the doorman began in excitement.

"Get after them. Two men. Stockings over their faces."

The policeman nodded and went out while the doorman propped up Vic as he sagged. Nothing like this had ever happened in all the years he had worked for the building. What he couldn't figure out was how they had got in. Every stranger was screened before he was allowed upstairs.

Vic described the slow opening of the closet door. He had probably surprised them in an attempt at burglary. They hadn't seemed to be armed, but they had certainly intended to rough him up. If it hadn't been for the telephone falling as it had, he would have been in real trouble.

The man from the patrol car was back. "They got away. Must have gone down in the service elevator as we came up in the passenger elevator. My partner never caught a glimpse of them, but they could have got out through the service alley around the corner. What gets me is that the door wasn't jimmied. So how did they get in?"

Vic shook his head.

"They were here when you came home?"

Vic grinned. "The doorman probably told you we had to carry in my friend Keith."

"Yeah. Anything missing?"

"I don't keep cash here. I don't own any jewelry. I have no art works. Aside from the furniture, there's nothing much to take."

"They just started to beat you up without provocation. That it?"

"Seems to be."

"You sure you didn't recognize them?"

Vic shook his head. "Their faces were hidden and they never spoke, so there were no voices to recognize."

"Did anyone know you were going to be out for the evening?"

"Everyone who knows me, I imagine, assumed I would be out. I attended the first night of *Forever and Yesterday* and went on to the party at Mary Smith's."

"Someone had a key to that door, Mr. Wales. This looks like a carefully planned operation. It strikes me that someone doesn't like you very much."

"That's how it struck me."

The policeman waited, but Vic seemed to have nothing more to say. "Not many people likely to do a thing like that," he suggested.

"Fortunately."

"You have any idea who engineered it?"

"A very good idea. But until I know for sure I don't intend to make any rash accusations. I don't intend to be sued for slander."

"Don't try anything on your own," the policeman warned him.

From the other room came a startled, blurred voice. "Whassa matter?"

"That your friend?" As Vic nodded, the policeman went to speak to Tom, then he left the apartment with the doorman. In a moment Tom appeared, hair tousled, eyes bloodshot, tie on one side.

"You all right?" He was trying to focus. "The cop said someone tried to rough you up."

"I'm all right."

"You look like hell."

"Just my leg. It will stop hurting in a few minutes."

Tom blinked his eyes to clear his vision, rubbed his hands vigorously over his scalp as though trying to clear his thoughts. "You need some pain killer. Where is it?"

"I don't have any. I knew this thing was going to be a long deal so I didn't dare become dependent on pain killers. Go back to bed."

Tom was concerned. "I'll call a doctor first. He can look at your leg, maybe give you something so you can sleep."

"I don't need a doctor. I've got to make a telephone call."

"Now?" Tom narrowed his eyes, trying to read the clock face. "It's nearly three."

Vic picked up the telephone and switched the button for an outside line. In Brenda's small personal directory he found the number he wanted. The phone was answered so promptly that he grinned to himself.

"Ralston? This is Victor Wales. Call off your goons. I don't scare." He set down the telephone.

"Ralston?" Tom said blankly. "You mean Ralston was responsible for this business tonight?"

"That's exactly what I mean."

"I don't get it." Tom was bewildered. "Why would Ralston be after you?"

"Because I'm after him. I promised Bill. For Brenda's sake."

"Brenda and Ralston?" Tom sounded stunned. "Ralston! But I thought it was Markham."

"If you are sober enough to take it in," Vic said, "I'd better tell you about Markham. It might at least prevent you from pulling another stunt like the one at Mary's tonight."

"How much do you think I can take?" Tom

demanded. "Though I'm sorry about all that. Seeing him so at home in our apartment set me off."

"Markham wasn't responsible for you bringing those people with you."

"What is this about Markham?"

Vic described Markham's call and summed up his statement.

After a long time Tom asked, "Did you believe him?"

"I believed him. Knowing how Mary felt about you, I never understood that business of her leaving you for someone else. It didn't hold water. You can rely on this: he was never Mary's lover. She simply stood by to help his wife."

"Why didn't she tell me?" It was a tortured cry.

"She wanted to be trusted. She had to be trusted. Or the whole marriage was dust and ashes. Personally I think that she had a somewhat exalted idea of marriage and she was demanding a hell of a lot."

Tom got up abruptly and stumbled into the bathroom where he was very sick. When he came out he stood looking at Vic. "I'm going to make some coffee. Sober up."

Somewhat to Vic's surprise he succeeded in making a pot of coffee and in bringing two cups, safely but rather unsteadily, to his room. After a few swallows of the bitter, scalding stimulant Vic discovered that he felt better. Tom, too, seemed to be wider awake, though he still left a lot to be desired.

"Perhaps the coffee was a mistake," Tom said at last. "You need sleep."

"I'll get it. I'm half asleep now."

Tom helped him undress and got him into bed. He turned out the light. Vic heard him go into his own room. For a moment the pain in his leg seemed to be unbearable. Then it faded. He turned on his side and slept.

## II

A woodpecker had mistaken Vic's skull for a tree and pecked away at it persistently. Someone with a blowtorch was working on his leg, sending flames up and down his shin. One of Ralston's goons had gripped his shoulder, pinning him down. Vic made a dim, halfhearted effort to escape, but it was no use. He was buried too deeply to stir. The sleep of death, he thought, and sank back into it almost gratefully.

The fingers tightened on his shoulder, shook him, and he turned his head, felt the stab of pain, sent groping fingers to explore the lump that felt as big as an egg.

"Mr. Wales! Mr. Wales!" Then the voice was speaking to someone else. "I can't rouse him. I'll have to call a doctor."

"But what happened? My God, look at this room!" That was Mary's voice, and Mary couldn't possibly be there.

Vic opened his eyes and saw Winnie bending over him, her kind face distressed; saw Mary, in the doorway, ashen with shock.

"Hello," he said.

Winnie's hand released his shoulder, took his wrist.

"Vic, darling," Mary exclaimed, "what happened to you? I've been calling all morning. Tom isn't here and Winnie couldn't rouse you. She said your room was a shambles, and it is."

"Time?"

"Eleven-thirty. What hap—"

He grinned at her. "Ralston sent some goons to rough me up last night. Looks as though they succeeded."

"Ralston!" She was surprised. She was not, Vic was now wide awake enough to realize, particularly interested. Whatever had made her telephone all morning, whatever had brought her to his apartment, had little or nothing to do with him.

"Didn't Tom try to help you or was he too drunk?"

"Too drunk." Vic told her about finding Tom at Helen's and bringing him home.

"Helen Manning! That's odd. Of course, she's very attractive if you like that cold type."

Only Vic's eyes laughed. "Whatever took Tom to Helen's, it wasn't for purposes of dalliance. He was out like a light. It required the combined services of a taxi driver, the doorman, and the elevator man to get him up here." Vic felt the lump on his head and winced. "Winnie, did Mr. Keith get off all right this morning?"

"Oh yes. He left a message saying he hoped you'd feel better and that you had better take it easy today." The maid turned to Mary. "He'll be all right, Miss Smith. Pulse nice and strong and steady. Though maybe I'd better call a doctor just to be on the safe side. That knock on his head could be a slight concussion."

"Just a sore head." Vic smiled at the two anxious women. "If you'll both clear out of here, I'll get up."

"Should you?" Mary asked, but she asked it eagerly.

Vic stared at her for a moment. She looked terrible. Mary who should be on top of the world with a smash hit. Mary who should be sleeping after the strain of last night's performance. She didn't look exultant. She looked—scared to death.

"Of course I should. Winnie will get us both some breakfast, won't you, Winnie? Unless you've already eaten, Mary."

"Eaten?" the actress repeated as though she did not know the meaning of the word.

When the two women had gone he got out of bed. He felt the way Mary looked. Terrible. His leg hurt. His head hurt. He was groggy. Concussion? He didn't think so.

When he came into the living room, after a swift shower and shave, from which he emerged in a thoughtful mood, he found Mary intent on the radio, the volume turned low. He stood watching her, unobserved. She switched impatiently from station to station.

"How were the reviews?" he asked.

The wide blank eyes looked at him without expression. "Oh, reviews," she said at last. "Fine! Fine! Glowing. Say it will outrun *My Fair Lady*. Vic—" She broke off as Winnie came in with coffee, shirred eggs, muffins, melon. When the maid had gone and Mary was seated Vic eased himself into a chair.

"What really happened here last night, Vic?"

He described briefly his encounter with the goons. If there were gaps in his story, she was not aware of them. "So what with the general uproar and the police prowling around, Tom woke up, made us both some coffee, and put me to bed."

"Well, you had a lot of excitement." She drew a long, shaky breath.

"There's something else," Vic said, and he told her about Markham's visit.

Her mouth twisted with pain. "That was like John," she said huskily. "He was terribly upset when you came to my apartment."

"Last night I told Tom all about it. I hope you don't mind. It's high time he knew."

"Did he believe you?"

"I think so. For a few minutes he was a very, very sick man."

Vic waited for her to speak, sipped coffee thoughtfully. He was sure now. "What is it?" he asked at length. "What brought you here this morning?"

"You loved me once, Vic. I never played on that, did I? I never pretended. But I wanted you to be happy. I was glad, more glad than I can say, when Bill left you his money."

"Even when you thought I had killed Bill?"

She did not answer. After a long time she pushed aside her untouched plate and lighted a cigarette.

"Are you going to tell me what brought you here?" There was no light in his eyes. "Because I loved you once."

"Because I need you, Vic. Something terrible has happened. Something so awful . . ." His stillness helped to steady her, to steady the voice that was out of control. "This morning John called me. He was frantic. Norma's nurse had found her in her room in a coma. They rushed her to a hospital, but there's not much chance of pulling her through. The doctor said she had taken an overdose of sleeping pills. But after the nurse talked to him he said she might have been given them."

"My God!"

"Because she was awakened about four-thirty this morning and called out and a voice said, 'It's Markham. Go back to sleep.' So the police came to John's apartment. They wanted to know where he had been. They think, if she dies, it will be murder."

She went to the radio. "Time for news. I've been listening all morning, but so far n-nothing . . ."

". . . according to the Secretary of Defense," said an impersonal voice. "A news flash just in. John Markham, former presidential adviser who resigned four months ago under fire over the Ralston contract for army clothing, was questioned this morning by the police in the death of his wife, which doctors believe to be the result of an overdose of sleeping pills.

"The discovery that Markham was married comes as a great surprise. Mrs. Markham was the former Norma Wellington, an actress some years his junior. She had been staying at the Connecticut house of Mary Smith, the actress, whose new musical comedy, *Forever and Yesterday,* opened last night. Miss Smith's name has been frequently linked with that of John Markham. It was at her house that Brenda Benton died by drowning last summer. Miss Benton, it will be recalled, refused to testify before the Congressional Committee that investigated the awarding of the Ralston contract, in which Mr. Markham was alleged to be implicated. Last night Miss Smith's husband, Thomas Keith, from whom she is now separated, attempted to fight Markham in the lobby of the theater but was prevented by a family friend, the well-known concert pianist, Victor Wales.

"The weather will follow this message..."

Mary switched off the radio. The fingers that she placed on Vic's hand were icy. "She's dead. Norma is dead."

"And the same cast is appearing in the new production," Vic said, "with Mary Smith cast in the leading role—her house, her husband, her friend, her—"

Mary made a small gesture and he was silent. At last she moistened her dry lips. "What is going to happen now, Vic?"

"Only God knows. But I hope to God your maid was in the apartment all night, Mary, because you are being given a terrific motive for killing Norma Wellington."

"I? Oh, don't be absurd. It's John who has been placed on the spot."

As the telephone rang Vic reached for it, thankful that there were so many extensions in the apartment. He wasn't sure he could have stood up.

"Vic!" Tom was hoarse with excitement. "Vic! Have you heard about Markham's wife dying up at Mary's?"

"Yes." Vic looked at Mary and shaped the word "Tom."

"I've been trying to get Mary and that thickheaded Swede maid of hers won't let me through. Says she isn't there. Of course she is there. Unless— do you think she has gone—"

"Mary is here."

"So she came to you right away."

"Oh, for God's sake," Vic said wearily.

"Sorry. I'm sorry. Vic . . ."

Vic raised his brows and gestured with the telephone. As Mary took it from him he pushed back his chair and, leaning on his cane, went into his room. He heard Mary cry, "Tom! Tom, darling. Oh, Tom!"

He shut the door.

## THIRTEEN

LONG AFTER MARY had left, the memory of the radiance in her face haunted Vic. He was torn by conflict. "I owed her that," he told himself, but a part of his mind demanded in horror, "What have I done?"

Winnie, moving with quiet efficiency, was straightening his room. She worked with none of the customary noise and confusion of cleaning women, who seem to feel that their worth is in direct proportion to the disturbance they cause. Now and then she made a little sound of distress as she gathered up pieces of the broken vase from the carpet, knocked over during last night's scramble, or found Vic's suits tumbled on the floor of the closet in which the two men had hidden.

When she came out of his room, removing her apron, Vic said in concern, "It's after two and you're not supposed to work here later than twelve. I hadn't realized the time. You should have told me."

"I couldn't leave the place like that," she said in her soft voice. "Anyhow, I gave up my afternoon job yesterday, so it doesn't matter."

"Gave it up?"

"Well, the—the lady was talking quite loud about niggers and her husband said, 'Don't call them that.

Winnie will hear you. It will hurt her.' And the—lady said, 'Oh, nonsense. You can't tell me they have the same sort of feelings we have.' So I left a note saying I wouldn't be back."

Vic grinned at her. "I'll bet it was a polite note too."

"Yes, it was," Winnie said gravely, and then joined in his laughter.

"I think you had better get us both some lunch," Vic suggested. "Then—do you like the country, Winnie?"

"I grew up in the country. It's home to me."

"How would you like to go up to the Connecticut house as my housekeeper? You could keep the place up for the time being, and if I should ever live there, you could have what help you need."

Winnie folded her apron carefully, refolded it, trying to conceal her tears. "That would be—fine," she said. Her fingers stroked the apron, dug into the pocket. "Oh, here's that message from Mr. Keith. I've already told you what was in it." She pulled out Tom's note. "You'll need someone here to take my place mornings."

"Perhaps you can find me someone and train her before you move up to the Connecticut house."

"I've got a cousin who has to work. Her husband was in a car crash and he's lost his job, truck driving. She is a right good cleaner and she could get breakfast for you, but she's not a fancy cook."

"You arrange it." Vic switched on the radio for the two-o'clock news.

John Markham was still being interrogated in the death of his wife, Norma Wellington. The word arrest was not used. Mary Smith had also been questioned at her apartment about Mrs. Markham's long residence at her house, but she refused to give any interviews to the press. Tom Keith, husband of the musical-comedy star, had seen reporters. He admitted that he had provoked a quarrel with Markham and said he intended to apologize. He had been drinking at the time and he held himself solely responsible for the scene in the theater lobby. Mr. Keith denied that he and his wife were estranged.

The telephone rang and he switched off the radio.

"Wales? This is Chuck Fedder." Vic held the telephone away from his ear to protect his hearing. "We've got to have that talk. Sorry I couldn't make it before. Never can get a minute to myself. Come along now, will you? Right away?"

"Your office?"

"God, no! The place is bedlam with those blondes milling around and pulling hair. I waited until Tom came back—looks as though he has patched things up with his wife, by the way. He seems to be on top of the world—and he can weed out the blondes. I came home to have some peace. Julie is here but she's lying down, so we can talk in peace. Say, did you hear about Markham's wife? Never even knew he was married. Something screwy there all right. And she died at Mary Smith's. That place must be jinxed and it's going to be bad publicity. I'm afraid Tom will leave us and go back to his old press-agenting job for her. She's going to need him, the way the news is breaking. Well, see you. Make it as quick as you can. Julie won't sleep all afternoon."

Chuck admitted Vic himself, grabbing his hand in spongy fingers. "This is swell. Come in. Come in." He tossed a newspaper off the chair onto the carpet. "Try that chair. Place is a mess. Our couple took off unexpectedly last night to visit a sick daughter, and this is the maid's day out. Wouldn't you know? How about a drink?"

He waddled across the room and mixed drinks, handed Vic a glass, and sat down—the operation was rather like launching a ship—with a sigh of relief. For all his noisy exuberance the look he gave Vic was rather uncertain.

"We got the bum's rush last night. First time I've ever been thrown out of a party."

"Whose idea was it?"

"Tom Keith's."

Vic's eyebrows rose.

"Well, Julie maybe had something to do with it. She's a businesswoman first, last, and all the time. She figured a lot of celebrities and a lot more people on the make would be at a party like that. In our racket you never know where you'll pick up a new client. And then it pays to be seen around."

"And why Ralston?"

"He took us to the theater. He couldn't very well be dropped later. So why he should blame us for what happened I can't see."

"Whose idea was it to leave Tom at Helen Manning's house in the Village?"

There was no mistaking Chuck's astonishment. "At Helen's! I'll be damned. We had nothing to do with that. We broke up outside Mary's building. I took Julie home in a cab. Ralston walked; he has an apartment on East Sixty-second, just a few blocks away. Keith took a cab. Matter of fact, we put him in a cab before we got one ourselves because he was practically out on his feet. We gave the driver your address."

Chuck's small eyes, embedded in fat, were intent on Vic's face. "How did you know he went to Helen's? What's going on between you two?"

"I took her home, walked to the door, and we found all the lights on and Tom passed out. I took him home with me."

Chuck grunted. "You had quite an evening."

"And that's not half. When I got home a couple of thugs were hiding in the apartment. They had come to rough me up, throw a scare into me."

Chuck set down his glass hard. "Who would do that?"

"Your friend and client, Horace Ralston. And the chief reason I came here this afternoon, Fedder, was to lay it on the line. Tell Ralston to keep off. One more move out of him and I'm turning him over to the police."

"Ralston," Chuck said thickly. "It's Ralston I wanted to talk to you about when Julie isn't around. Only what is his interest in you?"

"The same interest you had when you asked me to dinner the night I reached New York. I'm stirring up the Markham affair and people don't seem to like it. The whole boiling of you are scared to death of what Brenda might have told Bill Benton and what he might have told me."

A fat hand pressed hard on Vic's knee. "You're wrong," Chuck said, his jowls quivering with his earnestness. "We were fond of Brenda. Julie thought it would be a friendly gesture to ask you to dinner. That's all there was to it. If Ralston is making trouble for you, it has nothing to do with me. Absolutely nothing."

"Would it have anything to do with Mrs. Fedder? She was throwing around hints and warnings last night like confetti. Who were they aimed at?"

"I don't know, Wales. I'm crazy about that woman. I'd do anything in this world for her. I give her the best." He gestured toward the huge room, the paintings, the furniture. "The best. I buy her diamonds from Harry Winston. You can't do more than that, can you?"

"But?"

Chuck withdrew his hand and Vic had a sense of relief. The soft pressure had repelled him. Poor Julie! She paid a high price for the things with which her husband surrounded her, bought her. But at least she had been aware of the price when she made her bargain.

"It's not enough," Chuck said. "She wants more. She's planning to leave me, Wales. Leave me. And I idolize her."

"I'm not the Advice to the Lovelorn. What do you expect me to do about it?"

"Let me explain, Wales. There's something in this for you. Thing is, I've been noticing. Julie seems to be selling her bonds, cashing in on everything she has, getting together a really big stake. I got a look at her checkbook and savings deposit book the other day."

"You think she's planning to go off with Ralston?" Vic was deliberately brutal.

Chuck shook his head. "Nope. That's over. They were playing around for a while. I knew it, but I was afraid to lose her so I kept still, played a waiting game, hoping it would cool off. Then Ralston dropped her when Helen Manning came to work for us. I knew it by how Julie acted. Now that I can't figure, can you? Julie all warmth and Helen all ice. But there is something going on. Julie is frightened. She had hysterics after you came here and said Brenda had been murdered. I think she knows something about that Ralston deal. I can't see anything else."

*What would you be willing to pay to know the truth about the Markham case?*

"Suppose she is involved in it. What would you do, Fedder?"

"I'd stand by her," Fedder said promptly, "just as long as she stood by me. I'd back her all the way. But if she leaves me for another man, I'll put her behind bars. I'm not going to lose her to someone else."

"I don't think she intends to leave you," Vic said slowly.

Fedder brightened. "You don't?"

"Nothing to gain by it and a lot to lose."

Fedder rocked with the blow, bounced back with the resilience of a rubber ball. "Then why is she selling her bonds to get cash?"

"Has it occurred to you," Vic asked, "that the cash might represent her share of the Ralston bribe?"

The change in Fedder's expression astonished Vic. Slowly a smile widened on his face. "So that's it," he said in a tone of relief. "Just a business deal."

As Vic blinked at this reaction to Julie's chicanery Fedder asked, "How did you get wise to it?"

"Yesterday she offered to tell me about the Ralston contract deal. She promised to have all the proof I'd need by tonight."

"Why would she do that? I remember her saying that she'd be seeing you."

"She'd do it for twenty-five thousand dollars." Vic's tone was dry. "Nothing more personal than that."

"Well," Fedder said at last, "it's not another man. That's the main thing."

Vic shook his head in wonderment. "One thing I've learned in the past few days is to steer clear of women. Before I'd commit myself to the strangle hold of love I'd rather put my head in a noose. It's quicker and more painless."

Fedder laughed uncomfortably. "Well, what can you do? Anyhow, now I know what it's all about, maybe Julie and I can get on better."

"Suppose," Vic suggested, "you call her in now. She's a businesswoman. Okay, we'll talk business. All the cards on the table."

"Just lay it on the line?" Chuck asked after a blank pause.

"Can you think of a better way to do it?"

Chuck couldn't. He pushed his great wobbly weight slowly out of the chair, picked up a cigarette, put it down again. Obviously he was afraid of his wife, but he could see no alternative. Anyhow, it was apparent that he would rather face her in Vic's presence than alone.

"You had better explain to her that it will be safer for her to tell all she knows and tell it now. Remind her that Brenda would be alive today if she had told the truth. The first murder is the hardest. After that"—and Vic's voice was ugly—"it can become a habit."

"No one is going to hurt Julie and get away with

it." Fedder made his way across the room, a grotesque figure that seemed almost as wide as it was long, hesitated in the doorway, walked down a hall, tapped at a door. Tapped again.

His yell was more an animal sound than one that had been wrenched from a human throat. Grabbing his cane, Vic hastened down the corridor. A door stood wide open. Chuck was bending over a chaise longue, placed so it had a stupendous view of the park. He was clawing madly. On the chaise lay Julie Fedder, wearing a deep-red hostess gown, split on one side to show a beautifully shaped leg almost to the hip. Over her head and bust was drawn a plastic bag, twisted and held in place by her own weight as she sagged against it. Her hands were taped behind her.

Vic shoved Chuck to one side, lifted the limp body, and then jerked the bag up and off her head. Beside him Chuck was whimpering, "Julie! Julie!"

"Call a doctor," Vic said. He pressed his ear against her chest, but he knew there would be no heartbeat. Her lids were half raised and he could see the whites of her eyes. There was a fleck of blood on her nostrils, froth on her lips. Her skin had a bluish tinge.

Chuck hastened back. "He's coming," he said breathlessly. "Is she going to be all right?"

"She's dead," Vic told him quietly. "I'd say she has been dead for some time. At least an hour. Perhaps more."

"No! No!" The fat man fell on his knees, clasped his arms around the unresponsive body.

"Don't move her!" Vic said sharply. "You'll have to call the police."

Chuck's small eyes seemed to recede into his head.

"She was murdered, Fedder. She didn't pull on that plastic bag and then tape her own wrists together behind her back. The thing is impossible."

Chuck's arms dropped away from his wife's body. He collapsed on the floor like some obscene blancmange, his whole body quivering. After a look at him Vic went in search of a telephone. When he returned, Chuck had not moved, except that his forehead rested on Julie's thigh. He was crying, the loud, uninhibited sobbing of a child.

"You'll have to pull yourself together, man. The police are coming."

With Vic's help, Chuck got slowly to his feet. He fumbled for a large silk handkerchief and blew his nose with a trumpeting sound and then looked startled and ashamed, as though so much unseemly noise might disturb the dead.

"Listen to me, Fedder! You're going to be asked questions. Understand? They're going to want to know who let the murderer in."

Chuck wiped his eyes. "Let him in?"

"Pay attention! You've been framed. Can you get that into your head? The servants called away unexpectedly. You alone with your wife, whom you suspected of preparing to leave you. Unless you can find someone else, you're for it. How long have you been home?"

"About an hour," Fedder said dully. "I had just come in when I called you."

"Can you prove that?"

Chuck's wits were beginning to function again. "Sure. I have all those blondes as an alibi. I was looking them over. I stayed until Tom Keith got in; he eats up that kind of job. Who wouldn't?" He realized this comment was hardly decorous under the circumstances. "Anyhow, I came straight here from the office."

"Then you had better pray that Julie has been dead for more than an hour. You see it, don't you? Julie admitted her own murderer."

## II

There seemed to be an army of men, doctors, photographers, fingerprint men, technicians whose function Vic never discovered as he remained, at the polite request of the police, on a chair in the great drawing room, staring out at the park.

There was a great deal of purposeful activity but little noise and no confusion. Men spoke briefly in low tones and went about their business. Most of them looked with wonder at the three-story room. All of them took a long, curious survey of Vic, summing him up, prepared to recognize him another time.

And over the whole scene hung Chuck's frantic, slobbering grief. He cried and whimpered and moaned. Again and again he forced himself into the room where the men photographed and printed a dead body, and each time he was gently removed. He blundered around like a bumblebee, picking things up, putting them down again.

"I can't live without her," he told Vic. "I can't do it. And the office—why, the business can't survive without Julie. She was the heart and soul of it. My God, the blondes! She had all the details of that scheme in her head. Wales, call Helen, will you? See if Julie left any notes. Julie! My darling Julie. How could anyone do that to her? Do you think she suffered? Do you think it was quick? Ask Helen to keep the evening free, will you? We'll have to go over that Barker deal. He wants a couple of sharpshooters to put on TV, to dramatize a new hunting lodge. Or maybe Keith—Keith's got his wife, but I've lost mine. Julie! I'll give her a funeral that's the biggest . . ."

*My daughter—oh, my ducats.*

It was his own physician, the last to arrive, who summed up the situation in a quick, comprehensive glance, took Fedder firmly in hand, and led him upstairs to his own room. Half an hour later he came down.

"He's asleep. I gave him enough to knock him out for eight to twelve hours."

"Thank God," one of the detectives said fervently.

"See that he is not disturbed. He can't be questioned now. Tell the servants he is not to be bothered by anyone for any reason until he wakes up."

"Where are the servants?" the detective asked.

Vic explained. "Fedder told me this was the maid's day out and his couple went off unexpectedly last night to see a sick daughter."

"Very convenient."

"That," Vic admitted, "is what I thought."

"Know their names? Where they went?"

Vic shook his head.

"He'll need someone with him," the doctor said. "I'll arrange to have a nurse for the next eight hours. He should sleep through, but you never know with these excitable cases."

When he had gone the detective gestured to a young uniformed man sat down and opened his notebook. "Might as well start with you. I am Captain Fuller."

Vic gave his name and address. He had come to the apartment in response to a telephone call from Fedder. He had met Chuck Fedder and his wife only once before, when he had been invited to dinner.

"When did you get here this afternoon?"

"Fedder called about two. I must have reached here at approximately two-thirty, give or take a few minutes either way."

"Can you prove that?"

"Taxi driver, doorman who announced me, elevator man who brought me up, Fedder himself when he can talk."

The detective didn't ask whether Vic had spoken to Julie, which seemed to indicate that she had been dead before his arrival.

"What is your association with Fedder?"

"None at all."

"Do they often ask total strangers to dinner?"

Vic explained that he was a friend of friends of theirs, that they had seen in the paper that he had come to New York, and they had called him.

"Just a social visit then."

"Yes."

"Fifty thousand strangers arrive in New York every day. To get a mention in the papers—" The detective snapped his fingers. "Got it! I thought the name Victor Wales was familiar. You're the musician. The guy who inherited the Benton money."

"Yes."

"Benton—Brenda Benton—the Markham affair. Fedder was involved in that, wasn't he?"

"Music is my line, not politics. I wasn't here at the time of the investigation."

"But you knew the Bentons well enough to get all their money."

"Yes."

"Do you know Markham?"

"I have met him. He called on me yesterday."

"His wife died this morning." The detective sat back, staring at Vic. "Two men get their names linked in that old case and both of them have their wives die on the same day. Quite a coincidence."

"I don't think so either," Vic agreed.

"This Mrs. Markham had been living at Mary Smith's house. You know Mary Smith?"

"Very well."

"Horace Ralston?"

"I've met him."

"Did he call on you too?"

"No." Vic grinned. "Not exactly."

"Open up," Fuller said with his first trace of irritation. "When did you see Ralston?"

"Last night. He crashed the first-night party at Mary Smith's after the opening of *Forever and Yesterday*."

"And?"

"He was bounced."

"You're making me get this the hard way, aren't you?"

"Ralston arrived at the party with Chuck Fedder and his wife."

"Anything strike you?" Fuller said. "The people who figured in the Markham affair certainly gravitate together."

"I think," Vic told him, "this is part of the Markham affair, and I believe if we could have got here ahead of Julie Fedder's murderer we might have found evidence that would solve that case."

## FOURTEEN

"I NEED YOUR help," Vic said bluntly.

David Case picked up a pencil and tapped it on a blotter. "I didn't think you'd have the nerve to come to me for help."

"That is rather an unusual stand for a man's lawyer to take, isn't it?"

"I prefer not to act as your lawyer." Case ran a nervous hand through his hair, but his expression was not nervous at all and his eyes were steady.

"Then suppose," Vic suggested, "you regard the instructions I am about to give you as coming from the Benton twins."

"What are you trying to pull, Wales?"

"If you'll listen, I'll try to make the whole thing clear. I thought I could handle it alone, but time is running out. So I need you."

"Well?"

"As soon as I could get around on this bad leg I came back to New York with just one purpose in mind. To stir things up."

"Why?"

"Because that's what Bill wanted. He wanted me to find out how Brenda died. Why she died. I told you when I saw you before that he believed she had been murdered. I spread that piece of news as far and wide as I could."

"Well?"

"Not well at all. I stirred up a hurricane. So far there have been two attacks on me and one rather crude attempt to make me run scared. But that's not important. What matters is that two people have been killed, deliberately and brutally murdered, because I have begun to look into the Markham affair."

"You mean Markham's wife? I heard it over the radio at noon. A fantastic business. I never knew the man was married."

"And Chuck Fedder's wife. I've just come from there. Someone pulled a plastic bag over her head and tied her hands behind her back. Not a nice way to go. So this thing has got to be stopped and stopped now. I made a bad mistake when I held out on you in the first place, but there was something I wanted to accomplish and I didn't know how else to play it. Particularly after you made clear you wanted no part of me."

"I suppose there is some part of this I can believe," Case said. "But you are implying that the murder of those two women ties in with Brenda's death. If you are going to attempt to prove that Markham killed them, you can clear out of here now. I won't believe you."

"Time is running out," Vic repeated. "If you want to display these girlish tremors, you'll have to save them until later. Now let's get to work because, little man, you're going to have a busy day. First, get out that envelope I mailed from Wyoming. Don't read it now, but be sure to read it later."

"What's in it?"

"Letters Brenda wrote to Bill during the Markham investigation. They won't," he added as Case started to speak, "answer any questions. They are simply background for what comes next. What we've got to do is to stop this killing."

"You think someone is attempting to wipe out everyone who figured in the Markham case?"

"Not everyone. But I'm taped as the next victim, and if I am put out of commission, there will be no one to finish the job. That's why I need your help. We've got to have evidence and have it within hours. And first I'll put you in the picture, show you where I come in." As accurately as he could, he repeated the conversation he had had with Bill Benton the night before the latter had died.

Case listened intently. "But that was the raving of a sick man. His suicide the next morning proves it. You're barking up the wrong tree, man!"

"And the attacks on me?" Vic described the man who had followed him through Central Park and the attempt to run him down.

Case was impatient. "Talk about girlish tremors! A mugger in the park, a careless or drunken driver, and you build a whole script on it. If that's all—"

Vic went on to the two hoods who had got into his apartment the night before with the evident intention of roughing him up. The police hadn't thought he had an attack of girlish tremors.

"They didn't say what they wanted of you?"

"They didn't have a chance. But I'd be willing to wager my last penny that Horace Ralston sent them."

"Ralston!"

"He practically warned me after I escaped being run down. That happened, by the way, outside Helen Manning's house, and he was there at the time."

"And?"

"Ralston was at Mary's when Brenda was drowned. Julie Fedder was his alibi, claiming that he spent the time with her, but she's dead too. And I'm as sure as you can be of anything you can't prove that Julie was the one who set up the army contract for Ralston. She had a lot of money in the bank her husband can't account for. My guess is that Ralston's hundred-thousand-dollar bribe was split between Julie and some venal member of the committee. I saw her in a cocktail bar yesterday with Ralston; she was on the verge of breaking. She's been terrified ever since I suggested that Brenda was murdered. After Ralston left she came to my table and asked how much I would pay to know the truth about the Ralston affair."

"How much did you offer?"

"Twenty-five thousand if I was satisfied with the evidence she had. She promised to give it to me tonight, and that's a date she won't be able to keep, Case."

"And where does the murder of Markham's wife come into this?"

"That's the chief reason I am yelling for help. I triggered that killing."

"You!"

"I'm afraid so. Now let's get down to it, Case. I need a lot of information and I need it at once. Get all the help you need. I'll pay for it. Ready?

"First, I want to find Brenda's private papers. Have you any idea where she kept them?"

Case shook his head.

"Positive? She never dropped a hint about a special hiding place?"

"Hiding place! Are you trying to be the poor man's James Bond?"

"God forbid! But that has priority. I've got to find them and I've got to find them first!"

"I can't help you there. I haven't the faintest idea. Of course, you wouldn't think of anything as simple as a safety deposit box."

Vic ignored the lawyer's sarcasm. "They aren't in a safety deposit box. Next, I want to know how many people have alibis for Brenda's murder. The question didn't come up at the time. I want facts. Third, we'll need the same thing for Norma Wellington's murder."

"The police are handling that. Anyhow, she took sleeping pills. It would be hard to know what time the alibi was needed for."

"Then see if you can get hold of the nurse who was looking after Mrs. Markham. Find out what she saw and heard in the night; if she has any way of identifying the man."

"You are hell-bent on dragging Markham in, aren't you? Do you realize what will happen to Mary Smith's career if she is caught up in this? Her house involved. Markham involved."

"She is caught up in it, Case. Do you realize what will happen if she isn't cleared?"

"You're still in love with her, aren't you?"

"Suppose," Vic said, "we disregard my motives and get some facts."

"Such as?"

"Who has more money than he or she can account for?"

"You mean the Ralston deal? Have a heart, Wales! The government boys checked that for months and came up with nothing."

"And you have hours. But a detective at Fedder's said this afternoon that the people involved in the Markham case tend to gravitate together. You know people everywhere, at least Bill said you did. Start digging as though you were digging a foxhole under fire. Don't leave out anyone who had anything to do with the Markham setup."

"I do this on my trusty old abacus, I suppose."

"Next I want to know who started the rumors that caused the Markham scandal to break. They were planted. How could such a thing be managed?"

For the first time David Case looked as though he had got hold of something tangible. "Well, it could be done, of course, by priming a few key columnists, radio, TV men; or, less obviously, by hints dropped in bars and night clubs frequented by newsmen. I know some guys—"

"Get at them. At the same time you might see if the same person circulated the rumors about me, Vic the Violent, Vic the Improvident. They didn't come out of thin air. When Bill's will was made public there was a kind of underground stink."

"I wasn't too happy about you myself." There was a heightened color in the lawyer's face.

Vic grinned at him. "That was fairly obvious."

"I'll tell you one thing, Wales. Mary Smith and Tom Keith were delighted to know you had inherited. They couldn't have been more pleased."

"I'd expect that."

"Those alibis." Case began to scratch notes, pushed the paper across the desk. "Any more you can think of?"

Vic looked at the list of names: Horace Ralston, John Markham, Chuck Fedder, Julie Fedder, Mary Smith, Tom Keith. He unscrewed his pen and added the name Helen Manning. Then he got up.

"I'll keep in close touch with you, Case. Don't waste a minute. I'll probably have further instructions."

David Case pushed back his chair. "You ought to get the police on this."

"They are on it," Vic pointed out. "They are handling both the Markham and the Fedder murders."

"Wales, you expect me to help you, but you haven't told me the truth, have you? Even now."

Vic laughed. "That from a lawyer!"

## II

Ralston's office had closed for the day. After the phone had rung ten times Vic hung up. It was, he noticed, after six o'clock. In the telephone directory, in the lobby of David Case's building, he found Horace Ralston's home address, on the block between Fifth and Madison on Sixty-second Street.

The building was a converted town house with a short flight of marble steps leading up to an imposing entrance, an ornate metal outside door and a plate-glass inner one. There were, according to the bells, only two tenants. Ralston seemed to have the first two floors.

The man servant who answered the door said that Mr. Ralston had left town for a long weekend. If Mr.—uh—would leave his card . . .

Vic found a card to place on the small silver tray and turned to go down the steps. From the street he looked up quickly. A shadow darted out of sight of the lighted window.

"That, Mr. Ralston, was stupid," Vic commented aloud.

"This, Mr. Wales, is stupid too."

Vic turned to see the man beside him, a man with a bald head and a long nose. "Well, my friend from Central Park. I hoped I'd seen the last of you."

"That's mutual." The long-nosed man fell into step beside Vic as they walked toward Madison Avenue. "But you keep getting in my way. Please accept a small piece of advice. Keep away from Ralston. You're muddying up the waters." He covered his bald head with a snap-brim hat and ran forward to hail a bus.

Vic signaled a cruising taxi and gave the number of Chuck Fedder's office.

A cleaning woman was swishing a damp mop across the lobby floor. Only one elevator was still in operation.

"Where are you going?" the elevator man challenged.

"The Fedder office. Anyone still there?"

"Hell, everyone seems to be there. Don't they keep hours? Ought to have a union."

The door of the reception room stood open and Vic heard the uproar as soon as the elevator door opened. A harassed-looking woman sat at the reception desk drinking coffee from a cardboard container. The remains of a sandwich lay on a crumpled piece of waxed paper.

A couple of blondes, synthetic but attractive, sat in low modernistic chairs, chattering.

"So I told him, like it or not, I was walking out,

and what's more, I said, I'm taking this up with Equity. And he said . . ."

On the right, in a big ornate office, half a dozen blondes were parading slowly up and down, watched by Tom Keith who perched on the edge of a desk, also drinking coffee.

On the left, Helen sat at a desk in a smaller office, talking over the telephone and making swift notes. As she set down the telephone she recognized him through the glass door and came to open it.

"What on earth are you doing here?" she asked.

He motioned her back into the office, closed the door behind him, and stood looking down at her.

"Something has happened," she said quietly.

"Yes. You'd better close the office, Helen."

"We still have a few more girls—"

"Not tonight. Chuck would want the place closed. Julie is dead. She was murdered this afternoon."

She pressed a hand to her lips. "Oh no!" she whispered. "Oh no!" Then she pulled herself together. "I'll tell Tom. We'll close the office at once. Then I had better call Chuck."

"Wait a minute, Helen. The police are going to ask questions. They are going to want to know where you were during the early afternoon, where Tom was, where your friend Ralston was, and where you all were during the early-morning hours."

"Early morning?"

"When someone fed John Markham's wife an overdose of sleeping pills. Do you know anyone who could get hold of sleeping pills?"

"Julie takes—took them like popcorn." She sagged against the desk. "I had better tell Tom and get rid of the girls."

Vic eased her into a chair, alarmed by her color. "Do you have a drink in the place?"

"In Chuck's office."

"I'll get it." Vic went quickly across the hall.

Tom, looking young and buoyant, his eyes bright,

waved the coffee container in greeting. "Come to see my blondes?"

"I came for a drink."

"This is the place for it," Tom said cheerfully. "The bar's behind that bookcase. Help yourself."

"Close the office Tom, and come over to Helen's room. We've got to have a conference."

"Okay. Another half hour—"

"Now. And don't tell them to come back tomorrow. The office will still be closed."

"Closed?" Tom stood up slowly, a frown pulling together his startlingly black brows. "Chuck?"

"Julie. This afternoon."

"God! Okay, girls, that's it for now. Thank you for coming. I'll get in touch tomor—in a few days."

As the girls, their protests silenced by something in the atmosphere, went out, Tom came to open the bar. Vic poured two drinks and glanced at Tom who shook his head.

"I'm on the wagon."

Helen set down the telephone hastily as the two men came in. "Did he tell you?" she asked Tom.

"About Julie? Yes. But what happened? You mean she's dead?"

"She was murdered. Someone pulled a plastic bag over her head and tied her hands behind her back."

Tom shook his head. "I can't take it in. This is going to break Chuck. Hey, how did you hear about this?"

"I was there when the poor guy found her. And there's no point in trying to call him tonight, Helen. His physician doped him to the hilt. He won't wake up before morning."

"You were there," Tom said. "Why?"

"Fedder telephoned and asked me to come. He was upset about Julie. He thought she was preparing to leave him."

"My God, if the police get hold of that, they'll arrest him," Tom said, aghast.

142   SCARED TO DEATH

"Apparently he has an alibi."

"Vic," Helen said dryly, "is interested in ours. The only time I've been out of the office was for an hour between twelve and one. I had an errand to do and stopped at the Oyster Bar for a stew."

Grand Central Station. People waiting three deep for stools at the Oyster Bar. No checking that.

"You don't think Helen and I had anything to do with Julie's death." Tom was more incredulous than indignant.

"It's not what I think. The police are going to check everyone."

"Oh, I suppose they'll have to. Though if Chuck didn't do it, I'd put my money on Ralston. He and Julie used to be as thick as thieves. Then the affair soured." Tom grinned at Helen. "You made the competition too heavy for Julie. Well, Vic, what do we do now? I'll put up a notice on the door."

"I'll do that while you give Vic your alibi," Helen said. Whatever shock she had suffered, she seemed to have recuperated from it. She moved briskly across to Chuck's office, consulted his desk calendar, and began to dial numbers.

"Giving me privacy while I confess my sins," Tom said and grinned. "What are the times that the police will want to know about?" When Vic told him, Tom said, "You are my alibi for last night as I am yours. So far as this afternoon is concerned, after Mary and I made things up I talked to the police. She didn't want to, poor girl. Then, of course, I came here. I've been looking at blondes ever since. And how I've kept my mind on them I don't know. Because, Vic, it's all right. Everything is okay between Mary and me." He checked his exuberance. "How selfish can a man get! I forgot about Chuck. This will break his heart. He was infatuated with that woman."

"It's curious," Vic said, "that everyone is sorry for Chuck. I haven't so far heard any sympathy for Markham, and he lost a wife today too."

Helen came back, switching out lights. In her hand she had a piece of cardboard on which she had printed:

OFFICE CLOSED
IN MEMORY OF JULIE FEDDER

She thumbtacked it on the outside door.

"It's a pity," she said to Vic, "that you insisted on taking Tom home with you last night. He would have provided me with an alibi for the Markham murder at least."

"I'm sorry about that, Helen." Tom was genuinely contrite. "I can't imagine why I went there. I blacked out entirely."

"Oh, by the way, I'd like my key back, please." She held out her hand.

"Key?"

"How else could you get in?"

He fumbled in his pocket, pulled out a handful of house keys. "One of these?"

"That's the one." Helen closed and locked the office while Tom rang for the elevator.

"I ran into your long-nosed friend outside Ralston's house a little while ago," Vic said in a low tone. "He warned me off."

"I hope you'll heed his warning."

"We'll talk about that. I'm taking you home." He let her precede him into the elevator.

"Are you, indeed?"

On the street Tom said, "I'll leave you here. I'm going to see Mary. Tonight I'll see the show through. Tonight—" His face alight, he ran to hail a taxi.

# FIFTEEN

"MARTINIS all right?" Helen called from the kitchen.

"Fine." Vic went out to join her. With an apron,

not a decorative but a practical one, covering her dress, she seemed less remote. "May I help?"

"You can mix them if you will while I put the potatoes in to bake. Let me get at the refrigerator first, please. There's not room for two people to maneuver." She took out a steak and a package of frozen asparagus.

While she set a small table in the studio Vic mixed a pitcher of martinis. Until she was ready he prowled around the room, looking at the books, the record collection, the record on the open player. It was his own recording of the Waldstein sonata. He turned to find Helen watching him, a curious expression on her face. Then she took off her apron and dropped into a deep comfortable chair.

He put the drinks tray on a small table beside her, filled the chilled glasses, sat facing her. He raised his glass. "To better days."

"I can't take it in," she said. "Those two poor women murdered. I can't take it in. This has become a nightmare. It can't be coincidence that they were killed the same day, but what could they have had in common, what did they have to do with each other? According to what you told me, coming down in the cab, Markham's wife and Julie are unlikely ever to have known of each other's existence, let alone to have met."

"Helen, I've got to get it straight. Are you in the clear on this business?"

She set down her glass. "Do you represent the police, Mr. Wales?"

"I do not, Miss Manning."

"Then may I ask how this concerns you?"

"Don't be a hypocrite. You know that as well as I do, Helen. I've got you in my bones. I'm in love with you."

Color flamed in her face and then receded. "That's an old habit of yours, isn't it?"

He looked at her steadily. "If you mean that there have been other women, yes. If you mean falling in love with them, no. Only once in my life did I ever love a woman until I met you."

"Mary Smith," she said. When Vic made no reply she added thoughtfully, "I suppose you turn to me now because Mary and Tom have patched things up."

"Do you?" He was smiling. He took her glass out of her hand and drew her to her feet, into his arms. He tipped up her chin, looked deep into the clear gray eyes. "Do you?" He kissed her. When at last he released her he returned to his chair. "I'd better stay away from you."

Her mouth was still full and red from the pressure of his lips. She reached for her glass, her hand shaking.

"I love you, Helen. I didn't want to fall in love with you. I didn't want any emotional complications in my life. Never again. But it happened to me. Has it happened to you, too, or was that just—what do they call it?—a chemical response?"

"I can't be in love with you." Her voice was bewildered. "Not possibly."

"Why not?"

"Because I don't trust you."

He was smiling again. "I gathered that. And the situation is mutual, you know. There's a little matter of the revolver in your handbag, of your ubiquitous friend with the long nose, of your curious relationships with Brenda Benton and the Fedders and Horace Ralston. I'd give a lot to know which side of the street you are working and whom you are working for."

"All right, Vic, you asked for it. I am working for Uncle Sam. So is Joe Coke, my long-nosed friend, as you call him."

"Well, I'll be damned! The Markham case?"

The Markham case, she agreed. The rumors about Markham accepting a bribe, having a hand in rigging war contracts, had disturbed a lot of people. The fact that Markham had the confidence of the President, that he had had a voice in policy making at the top level, was even more alarming. When the fact that the Congressional Committee was getting nowhere fast became obvious, that it had unearthed no real evidence, that it was dealing mainly in conjecture, the government boys set quietly to work.

Helen had been with them for several years on undercover jobs when they decided to plant her with Brenda Benton. It had been well arranged, an accidental meeting at a party. Brenda said she was lonely without Bill; Helen said she was looking for a temporary place to live. It had been as easy as that.

"Why Brenda?" Vic asked.

"The hints we got kept going back to the Fedder office. No one really doubts that Ralston paid a bribe to the person who helped swing the contract to him. Personally I think Chuck is out of it. In his own peculiar way the man is honest. Anyhow, he has a big operation there. He didn't need the money. It would have been too big a risk. But Julie is—" Her eyes widened in sudden memory—"She was having an affair with Ralston and she would do anything for money, no matter how much she has. I think she arranged to get someone to swing that deal for Ralston and that she got a part of the hundred thousand."

"And who got the rest?"

"Not Brenda, if that's what you are thinking," Helen said quickly. "It's not just that she didn't need it. Anyhow, she'd have starved first. She was honest and she was loyal. That was her trouble. She was too loyal."

"But she knew about the deal?"

"She knew something. It stood out all over her. She looked guilty. She acted guilty. And she was desperately unhappy. Poor Brenda."

"But by keeping still she destroyed John Markham. That's the thing that sticks in my throat."

"You're sure of that, aren't you?" Helen asked queerly.

"The facts speak for themselves." There was a touch of impatience in his voice.

"I thought"—Helen sounded troubled—"Brenda knew he was guilty and kept still because she loved him."

"Markham says not and I think he would know. He was still deeply in love with his wife. I can't imagine a woman making a sacrifice like that for a man who had no personal interest in her. No, one thing I am sure of. Brenda believed she was loved. That's one of many reasons why someone is going to pay for this."

"Someone? You sound as though you know who it is."

"Yes, I know."

"Then why did you let it go on?"

His sudden smile lighted his face. "I had to find out where you fitted in, for one thing. You had me terribly confused. For another, there is a small matter called evidence. Helen, did Brenda guess about you?"

"No, but a few days before she died I told her what my real job was. She liked me and I hoped she would trust me. I told her how much harm she was doing by leaving this cloud of suspicion not merely over Markham but over the Administration, over the whole government. I tried to make her see this was more important than any personal consideration. I implored her to tell the truth."

"What did she say?"

"She cried for hours. Then she said that I was right but she couldn't do it without giving a fair warning. And then—"

"Then she wrote Bill saying, 'They've tried to kill me.' What do you know about that, Helen?"

"She was terribly upset, so I asked Julie for some sleeping pills. She sent Ralston over with them. That evening I was out. Next morning I had a terrible time rousing her. She swore she had taken only one pill, but I had to call a doctor and he said she'd taken a lot. He read her the riot act. I thought she hadn't been used to them and that she had taken more in the night when she was too dopey to realize it."

"But you didn't think she had tried to kill herself."

"No."

"And you never believed she had drowned herself deliberately."

Helen shook her head.

"Why not?"

"I don't know. It simply didn't occur to me."

"Why?" He leaned forward, covered her hand with his, removed his own quickly.

"Because—why, because I just know she wouldn't."

Vic leaned back, smiling. "And that is the case for the prosecution. She just wouldn't. Now all we have to do is to prove it."

"And now," Helen said, "tell me about Julie. How did it happen, Vic? Why did it happen?"

"She was scared to death. I'd been muddying up the waters, as your friend Coke told me. I was stirring up the story of Brenda's death. Julie was in too deep and she wanted out. She offered to give me the dope on the Markham affair for a price. She was going to do that tonight, Helen. So someone made sure that she wouldn't talk."

He told her about Chuck's conviction that Julie was collecting all she could before she cleared out. Actually what he found was probably her share of the Ralston bribe.

"Do you remember the way she talked at Mary's party? She was finished, and like the fool she was, she was issuing a warning. A fake telephone call got the Fedder's couple away from the apartment and someone arranged to see Julie. That is why she was home; that is why she was dressed as she was." His mouth twisted wryly. "Dressed for the kill. She admitted her own murderer.

"She wasn't an intelligent woman, Helen. Acquisitive people are rarely intelligent. Acquisitiveness is a special quality. I think she warned her partner that she was selling out to me."

"Ralston? Somehow I can't see him killing anyone."

Vic grinned. "He can give a good imitation of it." He told her about the hoods who had tried to rough him up the night before.

"But you don't know it was Ralston!"

"He gave me fair warning when that car just missed me outside your house, if you remember."

"That was a deliberate attempt to run you down, Vic."

He nodded. "So it was. And the night before in Central Park when I knocked out your friend Coke . . ."

"I asked him to follow you. Everyone was on edge when you came back, wondering how much you knew, what you intended to do about it. We didn't want anything to happen to you. Joe said there was someone trailing you. He was trying to warn you when you hit him."

"And that revolver you carried to Connecticut?"

"Mine isn't a particularly healthy occupation," she reminded him. "I have a permit for it." She added, "And I know how to use it."

"And what were you doing prowling around the house that night?"

"I saw someone out there with a flashlight."

"Why didn't you say so at the time?"

"I didn't intend you to know about me."

"Why are you telling me now?"

"I'm not telling you. I am warning you." Helen got up. "I'll put the steak on now."

II

When they had finished clearing up the dishes Vic asked, "May I make a telephone call?"

David Case answered at once.

"Anything to report so far?"

"I'm picking up some of the damnedest things." Case sounded excited. "The most important thing is that I talked to the nurse, the one who was looking after Mrs. Markham. She never saw the man who got there early in the morning. She asked who he was and he called, 'It's Markham. Go back to sleep.' And she did."

"Well, we're getting places! What are the police doing?"

"Oh, they'd talked to her first, of course. Markham is home. I don't mean he's in the clear, but at least he's out of durance vile for the time being. My own opinion is that the police can't swallow this dose. If it had been Markham, and he had been up to shenanigans, he wouldn't have given his name. This time someone has laid it on a bit too thick."

"Anything else?"

"I know a guy on the *Herald Tribune*. He gave me the queerest story about the Markham rumors. I don't know what to make of it. There must be some mistake."

"Somehow I don't think so."

Something in Vic's voice made Case say abruptly, "One thing I'm sure of now. You aren't getting involved in this mess because of the Bentons."

"Not altogether."

"Wales, I'm not going to pull your chestnuts out of the fire. I don't like the way this thing is shaping up."

"Neither do I, Case. Neither do I."

Vic set down the telephone, stared at a painting on the wall without seeing it, dialed another number. The telephone rang for a long time. Then a dull voice said, "Yes?"

"Mr. Markham, this is Victor Wales. May I see you tonight?"

"I don't want to see anyone."

"Please don't hang up. I'd like very much—" The connection was broken. "He won't see me," Vic said as he turned around. "He won't even listen to me."

"Why should he?" Helen poured coffee. "Cointreau? Brandy?"

"Brandy, please." He sipped coffee.

"Don't look like that," Helen said unexpectedly.

"Like what?"

"As though you were responsible. I'm sorry too. That poor man has had a horrible time, his career gone, now his wife dead. But you aren't to blame."

"You're wrong," he said. "I am responsible for her death."

"Why was she killed, Vic?"

He laughed harshly. "Love. No wonder you are afraid of it, Helen. Love's a terrible thing."

"I'm not afraid of it. You are. You are afraid of giving yourself. You are afraid of being hurt and disillusioned. You are afraid of being—committed."

"Am I?"

After a long time she laughed shakily. "What's happened to me?"

He kissed her again, the smooth hair, the closed eyes, the perfect mouth. "You are committed. And may God have mercy on your soul! No, stay here. This chair is big enough for two. And I thought you were the original iceberg. I need to have my head examined. When will you marry me?"

She was laughing. "Marry you? I wouldn't trust you out of sight."

"Don't let me out of sight. You see how simple it is?"

She touched the scarred hand with gentle fingers. "What are you going to do about that? You gave up too soon, Vic."

"How do you know?"

"I called your doctor yesterday. He said you should have started therapy at once but it isn't too late." She slid off his lap, disregarding his protests, and went to start the record player. In a moment the soft presto chords of the opening of the Waldstein filled the room. Though he held out his arms she remained beside the player until the adagio began. "You can't stop," she said fiercely. "Go see your doctor tomorrow."

"Tomorrow." He got up, reaching for his cane. "I have other things to do tomorrow, my darling." He went back to the telephone. David Case's line was busy. Next time he called Case answered.

"Wales, did you guess how this would shape up?"

"Yes."

"It all points one way, doesn't it?"

"Yes."

"The police have found out that Fedder's servants got a fake call to get them out of the apartment."

"That's what I supposed. I don't believe in that kind of coincidence."

"Ralston seems to have slipped out of town."

"I suspect he is hiding in his own house. At least he was there a few hours ago. I saw him ducking out of sight of the window."

"How deep in this is he?"

"Up to his neck," Vic replied promptly. "He's facing a prison term for bribery of a government official and he knows it. If no one is watching him, get someone on it. He can be dangerous."

"Julie Fedder had a whole lot of cash in a safety deposit box."

"So I assumed."

"Well," Case said with justified irritation, "if you knew everything, why did you ask me to find out?"

"We won't know everything until—"

"Until I get the rest of the dope?"

"Until Brenda tells us," Vic said somberly.

When he set down the telephone Helen was bending over the big fireplace, a long match in her hand. She touched it to the Cape Cod lighter and stood watching the logs catch.

"I'm cold," she said.

"And frightened."

She nodded. "Frightened. Julie Fedder. Poor little Mrs. Markham. Brenda. All dead. All murdered. And for what? So that one greedy man could get a big contract."

Vic shook his head, his eyes on the logs that had

begun to blaze and crackle. "The Ralston deal was like those logs. Without them—no fire. But there is something else. The match. Ralston never envisaged the fire. From his standpoint he simply took part in a business transaction, not ethical, certainly, but not, unhappily, as rare as we would like to think. When he found what he was involved in I suspect he was horrified. He did his best to scare Julie into silence; he tried to shut me up."

"And what will he do now? You told David Case he was dangerous."

"Ralston is bound to have another trick up his sleeve," Vic said slowly.

"What?"

"I wish to God I knew."

## SIXTEEN

ALL THE WAY home from Helen's house Vic found himself whistling exultantly the triumphant little march tune from *Peter and the Wolf*. He touched the scar on his hand, flexed the fingers. "You'll work for me yet," he told them.

For months he had lived with an obsession that had become, in recent days, a mounting dread. There was only one end to this road, disaster, inescapable and complete. There was no happy ending. But there was, at least this moment, the memory of Helen in his arms, answering his kisses. Out of the ugliness he had salvaged this. And he whistled Peter's tune with a kind of defiance.

As he had expected, Tom's room was unoccupied, the door wide open, the bed neatly made. Tonight Tom and Mary would complete their reconciliation. Vic's mood of euphoria faded. He mixed a nightcap and then poured it impatiently into the sink. In the room that had been Brenda's he undressed slowly. For a long time he looked at the photographs on the wall. Then he got into bed and opened Markham's *In the Public Interest*. It was nearly three o'clock when he finished it. How else could I have played it? he thought, and fell heavily asleep.

When he awakened he saw by the bedside clock that it was nearly eleven. The sound of voices made him sit up alertly. Then he recognized them. Tom was there, talking to Winnie, Tom with all his old infectious gaiety restored. In a moment he came in carrying a cup of coffee.

"Room service," he said cheerfully.

"You seem to be on top of the world."

"I am. Here's your eye opener."

"Thanks," Vic said, "but I think I'll take a shower first." He was pleased to discover that the long sleep had dissipated his fatigue, that his leg felt limber and painless. When he came out of his room he noticed that the table was set for only one.

"I had an early breakfast," Tom explained, pulling up a chair. His mood had sobered. "There was a lot to do this morning. I went to see Chuck to offer sympathy and all that and find out what he wanted done about the office. Then I came on here to pick up my stuff and thank you for your hospitality."

"How did you find Fedder?"

Tom shook his head. "That poor guy! He has simply fallen apart. I couldn't get any sense out of him. He kept crying. Then he'd say he was going to kill Ralston. Then he would plan a funeral that—well, if he carries out his present intentions, it will make a Hollywood funeral look modest. Then he would worry about his blondes. Then he would cry again. I tried to get it into his head that he could call on me for anything, but I don't know how much he took in."

"Have the police turned up anything yet?"

Tom handed him the morning papers. The Fedder and Markham murders occupied a lot of space on the front pages and they had been linked not only with each other but with the Ralston contract deal. That, Vic thought savagely, is going to give Ralston something more to worry about. There was, however, more caution than there had been in yesterday's news.

Charles (Chuck) Fedder was in a state of collapse and could not be questioned as yet about his wife's murder. Mrs. John Markham (Norma Wellington) had been staying for many weeks at the country house of Mary Smith. Because of her taxing role in *Forever and Yesterday,* acclaimed as the finest musical of a decade, the actress would not be interviewed until later in the day. Horace Ralston was being sought by the police for questioning in the Fedder case as he was known to be a close friend of both of the Fedders.

"I hope to God," Tom said, "the police will let Mary alone. She is terribly upset about the poor girl, though why she should blame herself I can't imagine. She was only trying to be kind. Just because it happened in her house—he might have waited, done it somewhere else."

"Markham?"

"Of course. Who else would want to get rid of his wife?" When Vic made no reply, Tom said, a touch of fear in his voice, "Who else? I swear to you that Mary is not in love with the man. There would be no reason . . ."

Vic pushed back his chair. After all, he wasn't hungry. "I have some telephoning to do. I didn't intend to sleep away the morning."

"I'll get over to the office and try to clear off some of the details." Tom went out quickly.

Vic dialed David Case several times before the line was free. Winnie had made his bed while he ate breakfast. Now she was clearing the table.

"What's worrying you, Winnie?"

"Poor Mr. Keith. When I let him in this morning he was so happy it did you good just to look at him, but it didn't last."

"When you let him in? Doesn't he have a key of his own?"

"He'd lost it, I guess." She shook her head. "Drinking makes people careless. And he's always losing things."

"He won't be needing it again," Vic said.

Winnie smiled broadly. "That's what I thought too. They are such a nice couple. It's not natural for married people to be separated like that. First thing you know they begin to look around for someone else, and then someone gets hurt." Her face sobered. "Gets awful hurt. And they are both mighty attractive."

When Vic dialed again, David Case answered the telephone. "You meant it when you said I'd have a busy day. And night. I got a couple of hours' sleep here in the office. Otherwise I've been on the telephone until both ears are permanently impaired."

"But you got what I wanted?"

"I've never been sure just what you want," Case said slowly. "But I've got the main outlines. I can see the picture. Only I still can't believe it. That Brenda of all people . . ." His voice broke. He was impersonal when he spoke again. "Anything else on your mind?"

"Yes, but this is going to be tricky, David." It was the first time he had used the young lawyer's first name. "Very tricky. What counts is the timing."

When he had finished speaking Case protested, "You can't do it that way. It's too risky."

"How else?"

"Tell the police what you know. Let them do it for you."

"They'd have cause for suspicion and that's all. It's not good enough. There's no proof in this case."

"You'll be a sitting duck, man!"

"It wouldn't," Vic reminded him, "be the first time."

"Then I'm going to be there."

"You can't . . ."

Case's voice was quiet but determined. "I'll keep out of sight. I won't spoil things. But this concerns me now. I loved that girl."

"Have it your own way. Just keep the timing straight. Not a minute before eleven-thirty. Is that clear?"

"That's clear." Case added, "Good luck, Vic!"

"Thanks. I'm going to need it."

That afternoon Vic made his arrangements and then he paced the floor. Half a dozen times he started to dial Helen's number and then set down the telephone. What good would it do? He felt like crying out with Brutus:

> O, that a man might know
> The end of this day's business, ere it come.

There was nothing new in the afternoon papers. Mr. Fedder had declined to see reporters. One columnist devoted his space to an account of some of Fedder's more fantastic publicity stunts. Mary Smith, at the time the paper went to press, had not been questioned.

The President had sent a personal message of sympathy to John Markham on the loss of his wife. That item held Vic's attention for some time. A reversal of opinion had begun to set in.

It was nearly six when Case telephoned to say, "The Ellises are moving out of the house now and just sent for a taxi to take them to the station. I talked to Ferguson. He says Mrs. Ellis is frothing at the mouth and intends to, and I quote, see the world knows that you have driven them out in the cold."

For the first time that day Vic laughed aloud.

At half-past ten he let himself out of his apartment. The Chrysler was waiting at the curb. That was according to his orders. What he had not expected was the sight of Helen Manning seated at the wheel. He stared at her aghast. Then he nodded to the curious doorman and got in beside her, closing the door so that their conversation might not be overheard.

"What are you doing here?" There was no welcome in his voice, in his eyes.

"I'm going with you, Vic."

"Going where?"

"The Connecticut house."

"How did you know? Did Case tell you?"

"No, my orders came from Joe Coke."

"Either my phone has been tapped or the apartment is bugged."

She was silent.

"So you know all about it." When she did not answer he said quietly, "Please don't come, Helen."

"This is my job, Vic. Anyhow—"

"Don't tell me"—his voice was lighter now—"that you are going along to protect me!"

"You needn't laugh."

"I'm not laughing." He slid his arm around her, turned her face to his, kissed her gravely. "I love you."

"When you say that, smile."

Unsmiling, they looked at each other for a long time and then she released herself. As the Chrysler moved away from the curb he felt the revolver in her handbag.

II

After they reached the Sawmill Parkway there was little traffic on the road. For some time Vic rode with his head over his shoulder. The car behind kept a steady pace, but it made no attempt to pass.

"We have company," he said at last. "Is that your friend Coke?"

"With reinforcements, I imagine."

"I hope they have brains enough to keep out of sight. They could gum up the works."

"They're going to play it your way as long as they can."

"Nice of them," he grunted.

It was a little after midnight when they reached the Connecticut house. Vic drove the car into the garage and closed the door. As he stood back, three matches were struck in rapid succession in the darkened apartment above the garage, but Ferguson did not appear. He had had his orders.

"We'll try the house first," Vic said as he unlocked the door.

Helen groped for the light switch and he checked her, his hand on hers. "We'll have to make sure first that all the curtains are closed," he reminded her.

They made a quick tour of the lower floor, drawing draperies and curtains so that no gleam of light could be detected from outside. They ended with the kitchen where Vic shed overcoat and hat.

"We might as well start here."

"Whatever there is can't be hidden on the second floor," Helen said definitely. "I've searched every inch of it, but I never had an opportunity to take a good look at this floor without being interrupted."

She added her Chinese red cape to the pile on the chair. For the first time he noticed that she wore dark slacks, sweater, and sneakers. She was prepared for action.

"I'll start with the kitchen," she suggested, "because I'd know better where to look."

"Okay, I'll take the long drawing room, and we can work around until we meet."

Vic had never before really observed the long drawing room, a gracious, livable room, oak paneled, with a big fireplace at one end, French doors that opened onto the lawn at the other, deep carpets, comfortable chairs and couches, some vivid paintings on the walls. All this was his. For all the rest of his life. His. Made possible by Bill Benton.

*Over to you.* Those were the last words Bill had spoken to him.

Vic inspected cabinets, table drawers, picked up cushions, surveyed in dismay the thousands of books on the shelves. If worst came to worst, they would all have to be examined, but he would search them only as a last resort.

*I've left them in the usual place.*

Vic went quickly through room after room. It was a youngsters' hiding place, he was sure of that; one of the secrets that had made the Benton twins a closed corporation. It wouldn't be subtle; it would be something that would amuse children, something to which they would have easy and unnoticed access.

He looked around the small living room, searched the desk, opened some ornate Japanese boxes displayed in a cabinet. In the powder room he spent more time. It was in the first-floor bedroom that he stopped short. On the bed covering there was the impression of a body, where someone had lain. Then he knew what had happened. The night he and Ferguson had missed the prowler, the latter had hidden under the bed until they abandoned their search and then had calmly lain down to rest until it was safe to leave the house. A cool customer. A very cool customer.

Twelve forty-five. He'd have to hurry. If he didn't find Brenda's papers first . . .

He barely paused in the big formal dining room. Young children would not have been permitted to play here. On to the smaller dining room, the pantries, with a panic sense of haste, which he recognized and tried to check. There was everything to lose by running scared. The swinging door to the kitchen opened and Helen came through.

"Good heavens! I've just finished the kitchen. You can't possibly have been thorough."

"I haven't. Somehow I don't think they are in the house. They must be outside."

"Outside!" Helen was dismayed. "There are ten acres of grounds and most of the place is landscaped.

We can't possibly search it in the dark. Not conceivably."

"Let's make our heads save our feet. Someone else has already figured the hiding place is outside."

"Oh, you mean the well."

"There's nothing in the well. Ferguson went down next morning to see. But it's that kind of place, I think. You've been here more recently than I have. You were here on Brenda's last visit. That's when she left this lot. Where did she go?"

Helen made a helpless gesture. "Everywhere. She sat on the edge of the swimming pool for a long time."

"Did she go in swimming?"

"No, I'm sure of that."

Vic considered it, shook his head. "I was thinking of something in an oiled bag hidden in the water, but the water in the pool is changed regularly. Ferguson would have spotted it."

"The playhouse!" Helen ejaculated.

There was a gleam in Vic's eyes. "Of course. You do have your uses, don't you?" He went back to the kitchen, brought her cape, and slipped into his overcoat, pulled a flashlight out of his pocket. According to his watch it was nearly one.

"Time's up," he said. "We've got to be cautious as hell from now on. Helen, stay inside, won't you?"

"You can't climb that tree," she reminded him. She switched out the light and they went into the small living room, pushed back the bolt of the door, and stepped out on the terrace. There wasn't a sound. No wind. Ferguson had raked the falling leaves, so that was no rustle under foot. There was no moon.

For what seemed to be a long time they stood side by side on the brick terrace, waiting for their eyes to adjust so that they would not need the flashlight. Slowly the terrace furniture began to emerge from the darkness, then lighter blobs on the lawn were revealed as white garden chairs. Trees took on shape. Crouching figures became low shrubs.

162    SCARED TO DEATH

> And in the dark how easily
> A bush becomes a bear.

Helen touched Vic's arm and pointed at the big oak near the driveway with a dark mass in the crotch of a lower branch. She pressed her revolver into his hand and he gave her his flashlight. She risked a quick beam that revealed a flimsy ladder against the trunk of the tree.

"Careful," he breathed in her ear. "It may have rotted."

"All right. Here I go."

She groped for a step and began to climb, feeling her way. Once there was a loud snap and she gasped, her foot scraped on wood.

"All right," she whispered. "One of the rungs was broken."

She was higher than his head now. Then she had pulled herself into the playhouse. The flashlight gleamed, moved from side to side, came to rest.

Standing with his head back, watching, listening, Vic was so intent that the bush had rustled several times before he was aware of the sound. Someone else was in the garden. He turned sharply. Then he remembered Joe Coke who had been close behind. He was probably watching now. Nonetheless Vic pulled Helen's revolver out of his pocket, held it ready.

The only rustling he heard now came from the playhouse overhead. Then there was a scraping sound, Helen began her slow descent. She missed the last step, lost her balance, regained it.

"Find anything?" he asked.

She reached into the capacious inner pocket of her cape. "It was in an old tin box marked, 'Warning. Do not touch.' There was a skull and crossbones chalked on it. I think this must be a diary of some sort. Anyhow, it's all there was." Her voice rose, louder, startled, "Who's there?"

As she spoke she switched on the flashlight. Mary Smith, caught in the circle of light, snatched the little book from Helen's hand and ran wildly toward the driveway where a car stood, its lights out.

"Mary!" Vic cried out. "Mary, for God's sake! You can't do that. Come back."

He broke into a run. Then someone grabbed his arm, jerked him around, knocked his cane to the ground. The revolver was snatched from his grasp.

Helen's flashlight came to rest on Horace Ralston who held the revolver pointed steadily at Vic.

"Stay where you are, Wales."

"Do you plan to use that thing? I thought you hired thugs to do your dirty work." Vic took a slow step toward him.

"Don't move!"

"How long do you plan to keep me here?"

"Until Mary destroys those papers."


## SEVENTEEN

THE SOUND OF the shot seemed to awaken the sleeping night and the revolver dropped from Ralston's hand. He clutched his wrist, his mouth opening and closing soundlessly in the white mask of his face.

"Okay, Vic," Tom called exultantly, "the Marines have landed. I got the bastard."

"Nice shooting."

Tom's head swiveled as he turned, tense and shocked. All of a sudden the lawn seemed to be covered with giant fireflies as men approached carrying flashlights. They had been concealed behind the bushes like the men of Birnam wood, Vic thought.

Joe Coke was standing beside Mary. He took the book out of her unresisting hand. "Thank you, Miss Smith," he said gravely.

Mary stared at him for a moment, her eyes like dark pits in her colorless face—all the faces were blanched out, giving the scene a curious unreality, as though it were ghosts and not living people who had filled the garden. Then she turned and ran to fling her arms about Tom.

"Tom," she choked. "Oh, Tom!"

One of Coke's men picked up the revolver Ralston had dropped, turned a light on his bleeding wrist. "We'll have a doctor look at that, though it seems to be just a minor flesh wound." He took Ralston's arm.

Ralston wrapped a handkerchief awkwardly around his wrist with his left hand. "What do you think you are doing?" he blustered, trying to free himself from the government man's hold.

"We're going to ask you some questions, Mr. Ralston, and this time we're going to get some answers."

"I have nothing to say except in the presence of my lawyer."

"Two people have been murdered to prevent them from talking, Mr. Ralston," Coke said quietly.

"I had nothing to do with that!" Ralston's voice was sharp with fear. "Nothing."

"Brenda Benton knew the truth about the awarding of the contract, didn't she?"

Ralston stood grimly silent.

"She was persuaded to talk, in the public interest, but she wanted, first, to issue a warning. That night she got an overdose of sleeping pills, which were provided by Mrs. Fedder but delivered by you to Miss Benton. Correct?"

"I merely handed her the bottle. I never went inside the apartment."

"Now that's odd. According to the maid who takes care of the apartment, someone had been—shall we say with Miss Benton at the time she fell asleep?"

Vic stirred. Winnie hadn't told him that, though she had given some oblique hints.

"I wasn't there!" Ralston's voice was suddenly loud in the night.

"Next day you just happened to crash a party of

Miss Smith's—that's rather a habit of yours, isn't it, Mr. Ralston?—at which Miss Benton was drowned."

"I barely talked to the girl!"

"It's unfortunate that your only alibi was provided by Mrs. Fedder who is no longer able to testify in your behalf."

"But, good God, it's true. Julie and I wandered around, talking, because Markham showed up. I didn't want to meet him any more than he wanted to meet me. We kept apart. That's all there is to it. And, anyhow, Brenda went off to swim."

"Where she was out of sight, around that curve in the beach. It would have been so easy to saunter off in that direction, to have signaled to her, to have held her down so that she drowned. Wouldn't it, Mr. Ralston?"

Ralston loosened his collar. "I didn't do it. I didn't —I want my lawyer."

"Then we come to Mrs. Fedder. You had a quarrel with her in Quilp's Cocktail Lounge the other day." When Ralston made no reply Coke said gently, "It was overheard, you know. Mrs. Fedder seemed to be afraid of you. I understand you threatened her."

"I . . ." Ralston swallowed, mopped his head, though the night was chilly.

"Later she promised Mr. Wales to give him the evidence he wanted on that contract deal you made. She was going to do that last night. But she wasn't able to keep that appointment, was she, Mr. Ralston?" After a pause he repeated, "Was she?"

Ralston's face hardened. In the white light of the torches all the faces seemed to Vic like tragic masks. "I didn't kill her," he said hoarsely.

"At Miss Smith's party, after her opening night, which you also crashed, Mrs. Fedder made some comments that might have sounded a warning. Do you agree with me?"

No reply. Coke did not seem to expect any.

"And yesterday someone made an appointment at her apartment, after the servants had been conveniently removed, pulled a plastic bag over her head, and took away the evidence about your contract, which she had prepared for Mr. Wales."

Ralston turned, disregarded the pressure of the government man's hand on his arm. "You—" he began, glaring at Vic.

"And that brings us to the men you sent to carry a —shall I say a warning?—to Mr. Wales."

Ralston managed a smile. "Prove it."

For the first time Vic spoke. "Those goons had a key to the place. When they reported back they probably returned it."

A breathless few moments passed while a struggling, cursing Ralston was searched. Then Vic looked over a half-dozen keys, picked one out.

"That fits my apartment door." He drew from his pocket a matching key.

"Well, Mr. Ralston?" Coke's voice was still gentle. "There's quite a score mounting up, isn't there? Two murders—an attempt—"

"I had nothing to do with the murders! I swear to God I had nothing to do with them."

"Now that's odd when you consider that these women were killed to prevent them from talking about your activities."

Ralston's self-assurance dissolved. "I didn't know. I didn't know. When Wales came East and said that Brenda had been murdered I was stunned. Julie called me that night. Stunned, I tell you. I'd never dreamed of anything like that."

"When you made the deal, you mean."

This time, as Ralston knew from the uncompromising faces, there was no way out. "Okay, I can tell when the odds are against me. This will wreck me, but it's better than a murder charge. Julie Fedder rigged that deal for me."

Ralston had met the Fedders at a party somewhere and had become a client of theirs. Fedder was expensive, but he got results. Ralston's public image, he assured them gravely, began to take on stature, to grow in importance. Minor labor problems and personal—entanglements—were kept out of the press. He and Julie had drifted into a casual sort of affair, not important to either of them, but pleasant, and then it naturally cooled off. Before that took place, Julie had come up with the idea of the government contract. She knew a member of the purchasing committee slightly and he could be had. So, okay, it wasn't according to Hoyle, but he wasn't the only one who played an ace when it was dealt to him.

"Even," Coke suggested, "when it was dealt out of the cuff."

Ralston shrugged. "Julie got in touch with her man and came back to say he could swing the deal but he wanted a hundred thousand. That damned hundred thousand the government boys found out about."

"Who got that money?" Coke demanded.

"I don't know."

"Oh, come now!"

"That's true. My own suspicion, and it's a pretty sound guess, is that Julie took half. But as for the guy she made the deal with, I don't know. She refused to tell me. I'll have to admit that when rumors began to circulate that it was Markham I was staggered. He was the last man in the world I'd have thought of. And he wasn't Julie's sort. I couldn't see her getting close enough to him to make such a proposition.

"Julie was amused about the whole situation, except, of course, she didn't like having the Fedder outfit involved. So I accused her of spreading the rumors about Markham herself because the investigators were getting too close to her boy. And she said it was true she had been worried but she wasn't the one who had done it. That was—"

Ralston came to a full stop, his eyes, startled and searching, moving from face to face. "You've got to protect me."

"It was the man who gave you the key to my apartment, wasn't it?" Vic said.

"Yes, it was Tom Keith."

"All right, Keith," Coke said. He added sharply, "Where is he?"

Tom Keith had disappeared in the darkness, taking Mary with him.

II

Coke issued orders sharply. Ralston was to be taken back to New York in custody. He scarcely protested and then only as a matter of form. The relief of escaping a murder charge made whatever lay ahead seem endurable.

Road blocks were set up. Keith couldn't have driven away, Coke said, because David Case had blocked the roadway with his own car. The knowledge that Keith had become Brenda's lover as his surest way of silencing her had roused a bitterness in the usually mild lawyer that made him more formidable an enemy than the grim-faced men who were consolidating their lines, moving in for the kill.

Vic stood watching the men scatter, searching the garage, the wide sweep of lawn and garden. Then he strolled quietly to the terrace where he and Helen had stood earlier and slipped into the small living room where a man was busy at the telephone.

The latter looked up sharply and then, as he recognized Vic, he nodded and went on talking. ". . . those descriptions go out at once. Anyone is apt to spot Mary Smith, at least." He put down the telephone. "Well, Joe was right. You really pulled a rabbit out of your hat. Only why wouldn't you leave it to men who are trained to do the job?"

Vic shrugged. "Suppose I had told you that Brenda Benton left some sort of record. Suppose you had found it. Would you have had an airtight case if Tom Keith hadn't virtually confessed by running away? All we'd have had would have been probabilities. Another thing, unless he had found himself over a barrel Ralston would never have cleared Markham."

"How could you be sure that Case's telephone calls would bring them all up here?"

"They had no choice," Vic pointed out. "They had to have Brenda's diary."

"Well, it's clear enough now. And once we know where to look we'll turn up the evidence."

"The one thing you took on yourselves was guarding Keith, and he got away."

He didn't like that, but his confidence was unshaken. "Not for long."

"He has his wife with him."

"Keith wouldn't hurt her."

"Wouldn't he? He has killed before. He is finished and he knows it. Personally—and I've known him nearly all his life—I can't see him surrendering tamely, facing life imprisonment, and leaving Mary free to rebuild her life with another man, particularly when that other man would quite probably be John Markham, whom he has made a career of destroying."

Vic's terrible urgency made the other man gasp, "My God!" as he headed for the terrace at a run.

Vic walked heavily through the brightly lighted rooms of the lower floor and finally climbed the stairs as though he were very tired. One by one he opened the bedroom doors, switching on lights. When he turned on the light in the corner room where he had once slept, he stood motionless for an instant. Then he went in and closed the door behind him.

Mary sat slumped on a chair in the alcove. All the emotion had drained from her face; her hands lay loose on her lap. Her eyes were dull. Tom turned from the window where he had been watching the search. The gun in his hand was steady.

"I'm not armed," Vic said. He turned his head. "I'm sorry, Mary."

"How did you guess where we were?" Tom asked.

"You seem to follow the same pattern. When you came up here the other night you hid in that downstairs bedroom, and tonight there wasn't any place else to go, was there?" When Tom made no reply Vic said, "There's no place to go now. It's all over. You understand that, don't you, Tom? They've got the whole story now."

"What story?" Tom was smiling.

"The story Julie Fedder told me the day before you killed her. You tried to punish Mary by having a little affair with Julie who told you the truth about the Ralston deal, partly because Ralston had broken with her, partly because she was afraid the committee was getting too close to the man she had worked with. You saw your opportunity so you stepped in and started rumors—you were always a smart press agent—that Markham was the man. A story," Vic went on deliberately, "that will clear Markham's name completely and set him back on his pedestal, perhaps even raise it a couple of notches because he was so ruthlessly victimized."

The smile left Tom's face. His hand shook; his finger trembled on the trigger. Perspiration trickled down Vic's neck inside his collar, but his eyes never released Tom's. Death hung by a thread, and the only chance he had was to hold Tom's attention.

"And the thing that is going to drive you crazy for the rest of your life is the knowledge that it was all for nothing. Because you misunderstood the situation between Mary and Markham you set out to destroy him. Then to protect yourself you began to kill, senseless, wanton, vicious killing."

"So you've been playing a game with me all the time," Tom said. "I wondered when you refused to drink the coffee I brought you this morning. It was all right, you know."

"After you doped the coffee the night Ralston's goons came to work me over I wasn't taking any chances. You set up that whole thing, didn't you? Told Ralston I was gunning for him, gave him the key, and went off to Helen Manning's so you would have an alibi whatever happened. Then I found you there and took you home. When I told you I knew Ralston was responsible and told you that pitiful story of Markham's wife to show you that he was in the clear, you couldn't stand it. Markham had to be destroyed. Not just because of Mary, but because Markham is the biggest, the finest person you know and you couldn't bear that. Could you? So you lit out to kill his wife with the rest of the sleeping pills, those left over after you had doped Brenda, trying to kill her. You wanted to kill Norma Wellington for the filthiest, most flimsy reason I've ever heard of, to set Markham up as her killer."

"I was afraid of that," Mary cried, "but Winnie said Tom had been there with you all night. She gave you his message..."

"A written message."

"What I can't forgive you for, Vic, is letting—last night happen."

"I wanted you to have something to remember, Mary. If I was wrong, I am desperately sorry."

"Perhaps you weren't wrong. Just kind."

They spoke to each other as though Tom were not there, as though he had already become a part of the irrevocable past.

"Why did you come tonight, Mary?"

"There was a call for me at the theater after the performance. Ralston said David Case had told him Brenda left some sort of record up here that would destroy Tom as well as him. He said he'd keep Tom in the clear if I would get it for him. He wouldn't be admitted to the house, but I was known here. So ...." She flung out her hands. "I knew it was wrong. But I loved him, Vic!"

"Mary!" That was Tom's voice.

She did not look at him. "I've suspected for a long time. One day I went to the Bentons' apartment. Winnie, Brenda's maid, was there. She gave me hints about you and Brenda, mostly, I think, because she was fond of Brenda, wanted to protect her. That was during the investigation, so I guessed then that you were the one who was keeping her quiet. And then I guessed why."

Tom looked at her, looked away.

"Then when Julie died everyone assumed that you had been with me, but we had only talked on the telephone while I was at Vic's. So I was terrified. But then—when Norma was killed and I thought you had been with Vic, I began to hope I'd been mistaken about the rest."

Tom turned to Vic. "Very, very clever. But you haven't fooled me for a minute. You've built this thing up, brick by brick. My jealousy of Markham— that's been your theme from the beginning. Has it occurred to you that there's another side to this case for your friends outside to consider? Your jealousy of me. You've always been in love with Mary. Bill saw that. Why didn't I? Because I trusted you, I guess. You made a will leaving everything to her."

Mary was startled. "Did you, Vic?"

He nodded. "Sooner or later this had to happen, and I was afraid you'd be caught in the crossfire, that you'd be hurt professionally by the scandal. I wanted you to have something."

Tom laughed. "You've set up as pretty a frame as I've ever encountered. For what? To get me out of the way, to clear the path for you—and Mary. Well, I've got her, Vic. If I go—she goes. I'm not going to be taken alone."

Behind Vic the handle of the door against which he leaned moved noiselessly, turned back again. He moved away from it, walking slowly toward Mary, so that Tom turned, too, following him with the gun.

"Keep away from her!"

Vic dared not glance toward the door. He took another slow step. Another.

"Shooting me won't help you, Tom."

"Nothing can help me now. I know that. You've got me cornered. But you're not going to walk out of here as I've seen you walk off a concert stage to shouts and applause. No one is ever going to stop you on the street again to ask for an autograph. No one is ever—"

The door was opening slowly, slowly. Something moved in the opening, reached out. Vic recognized his cane. It was raised and crashed down on Tom's arm. The revolver went off, Tom shouted, Mary screamed, and Helen flung open the door.

Outside there were raised voices, shouts, pounding feet. Vic lunged forward, kicked away the revolver, and flung himself at Tom. It was ugly fighting, smashing viciously, pounding each other, fists crashing into faces, fingers clawing at eyes. A table was overturned. A lamp crashed to the floor. Then both men went down with a thud that shook the room. Tom's hands were on Vic's throat, tightening. Then Vic dragged away one arm, began to twist it behind Tom's back.

With a tremendous push Tom heaved himself up, breaking Vic's hold. Vic tried to see, but he was blinded by the blood pouring down his forehead. He pitched forward on his face.

## EIGHTEEN

"NOBODY COMES in here," Ferguson said. "The man was shot. He bled like a stuck pig. Nobody."

"He got a trivial scalp wound." That was Coke, sounding impatient. "They always bleed. Let us in or, so help me, I'll have you arrested for obstructing justice."

Vic laughed. "Okay, Ferguson. The doctor says I'll live. Let them in and get us all some drinks."

"No drinks for you. Doctor's orders."

"Hey, where is that doctor? We'll see about that."

"He's still with Miss Smith. She fainted. Doctor says she is in shock and she had better not be moved tonight, so we put her in Mrs. Ellis's room. Miss Manning will stay with her."

When Ferguson returned with drinks, Case accompanied him. "I thought you might want a lawyer." He looked around the room. The place was a shambles and the blood had not yet been cleared away. "Quite a scrap!" He turned to Coke and the man with him who was busy setting up a tape recorder. "The doctor said you could talk now if it is necessary, but I'm sure these gentlemen would be willing to wait until morning, if you prefer."

"Let's get it over with," Vic said wearily. "What about Tom?"

"They're taking him back to New York," Coke said. "Very quiet and subdued. Stunned. As though he couldn't believe that he had lost. What put you on the right track, Wales?"

"Tom himself," Vic said slowly. "From the very beginning there he was in the center of the picture."

"What I can't figure out is, if he had no part in the Ralston deal, what was he trying to do?"

"Destroy John Markham. You know about Markham's wife and how Mary offered her house and another opportunity to cure the poor girl. Well, Tom walked in one night, found Mary and Markham together, and drew the wrong conclusion. Mary, mistakenly, I think, refused to defend herself. She told Tom not to come back until he trusted her.

"Tom had just one thought in mind. He was going to break Markham. To punish Mary he had an affair with Julie Fedder, who was easy meat, and found out about the Ralston deal from her. Julie was getting worried for fear the man she had worked with on the purchasing committee would be detected. So Tom saw his chance and began to drop hints that Markham was the man."

Case nodded. "I couldn't believe it when I began checking with guys I knew on newspapers and at the broadcasting stations. Every time we traced a rumor back to its source it came from Tom Keith. And I found"—Case looked at Vic—"that he had dropped those stories about you being hard up, so you needed

SCARED TO DEATH 175

Bill's money. I remember now he said something like that in my office the day I read Bill's will."

"I couldn't sign checks for a few weeks while my hand was healing, so the bills mounted up. Tom knew that. So did my creditors, so no harm was done."

Coke's partner made an adjustment to the tape recorder and Vic went on. Brenda Benton had become disturbed by the rumors involving the Fedder outfit in the Ralston contract. At length she went to Julie and demanded the truth. Julie told her she had better ask Tom Keith. All this, Vic said, Julie herself had told him during their curious interview in the cocktail lounge.

"Well, Brenda wasn't the kind of person who could be bribed or frightened into keeping still. But she was young and lonely and romantic and emotionally starved. So Tom took the surest, most direct way to silence her. She fell in love with him, of course." Vic went on heavily, "Probably she had been in love with him for a long time. He persuaded her that he was justified in destroying Markham."

Vic looked up to say, "You'll find all this in Brenda's diary." He handed the little book to Coke. "Thanks for letting me read it."

"We owed you that much," Coke said. "Go on and finish this. Then you can get some sleep."

Helen Manning, Vic continued, persuaded Brenda that she must tell the truth, and Brenda warned Tom that she was going to do so. That night he gave her a heavy dose of sleeping pills. Next day, when his first attempt had failed, he lured her away from her party and drowned her. The day after Brenda died he went out to Sheridan because he realized that Brenda always confided in Bill. He had to find out how much Bill knew, how much he suspected.

Coke held up his hand. "You say Keith killed Brenda Benton, Norma Wellington, and Julie Fedder. It would be comforting to have one single bit of proof."

"You need only one murder," Vic told him.

"What do you mean by that?"

"I mean the murder of Bill Benton. I saw Tom shoot him just before he shot me."

II

Ferguson scowled as Vic pushed open the kitchen door and sat down at the table where the caretaker was drinking coffee and listening to the radio.

"Who told you that you could get up? You look like a Turk in that turban."

Vic grinned and sat down with a grunt.

"How's your leg?" Ferguson asked anxiously.

"Oh, stop being such an old grandmother! What I need is coffee and some bacon and eggs."

"Fine. You might double that order."

Vic turned around to wave at David Case. "Morning, David. What am I running here, a hotel?"

"I thought I'd better stay on in case of any complications. Miss Smith is better. She's going back to New York in a few hours."

"Is Miss Manning still here?" Vic hoped his voice was casual.

"Yes. She was up with Miss Smith all night and she must have had a rough time of it. I could hear Miss Smith crying and carrying on."

While Ferguson brought the coffee and busied himself at the stove, Vic turned up the volume of the radio. The Ralston case was back in the news with a vengeance. Ralston was being held for the grand jury. John Markham had been cleared of all complicity in the Ralston scandal. The President had made a personal telephone call asking him to return to Washington. Mr. Markham was not available to reporters, but a spokesman had declared that he would probably answer the President's summons after his wife's funeral.

Thomas Keith, husband of the famous musical-comedy star, Mary Smith, had been arrested and charged with the murder of William Benton. He was also being questioned about the murders of Mrs. Charles Fedder and Mrs. John Markham. The police had promised to issue a statement later in the day.

"So where do we go from here?" Vic pushed back his plate.

"You ought to eat something," Case advised him. "They'll be around with more questions some time today."

"I'm not hungry. Stop bothering me."

"You pulled it off," Case insisted. "You ought to be feeling good."

"Good! For twenty years Tom was the closest friend I had in the world. Good!"

"Are you really sorry for him?" Case spoke with a kind of wonder, his eyes on the signs of that savage struggle of the night before.

"You can't wipe out the past in one minute."

"He could," Case reminded him. "He did. The most ruthless—"

"He was jealous," Vic said, "not only of Mary, but of her success. And when you come to think of it, we all had more than he did. Bill was a fairly rich man. I had done well with my profession and got off to an early start. But neither of us was aware of how he felt because—well, because he had Mary. That should have been enough for any man."

"When did you first suspect him? Oh, of course, when he shot Bill and you."

"No, it was actually the night before." Vic broke off to say, "I've tried to do what Bill expected of me, but my primary intention all along has been to clear Markham if I could. To my mind he's a necessary man and I couldn't believe in his guilt.

"Well, Bill was worried about Tom. That was like him, you know. Facing a hell of a death himself, but worried about someone else. He was afraid Tom was the kind to kill himself over Mary. I couldn't see Tom killing himself, and the revolver Bill had found in Tom's luggage was Bill's own weapon. I began to see a picture of Tom jealous of Markham; of Brenda placed in a key position to know the truth about that contract and vulnerable to Tom's special charm for women. If he had been seeing Brenda, it would have been easy for him to get hold of Bill's gun. I began to wonder.

"That night I saw Tom retrieve the revolver. In the morning he shot Bill and killed him, shot me but missed a vital spot."

"But why?"

"Because he couldn't afford to have any investigation into Brenda's death. Julie would begin to put two and two together. All that saved me that morning was the proximity of the Rangers. Tom had to run like hell to be found far enough away from the tent to avoid suspicion. I managed to get Brenda's letter from Bill's body before I fainted."

"Why didn't you accuse him of the shooting at the time?" David demanded.

"Because," Vic said with unwonted seriousness, "this country needs Markham. It's not altogether a matter of needing his judgment, his sound advice, his far-reaching vision. As a people we need to have our faith in his integrity restored. Markham wasn't the one who lost most by that scandal. The people lost, the President lost, the whole democratic system lost when we began to question the soundness of its foundations. And I knew Tom well enough to feel sure that, unless we got him dead to rights, he would drag Markham down with him. I just didn't know any other way to play it.

"As soon as I got back to New York he moved in on me to see what I remembered of the shooting, what I was up to, what I intended to do about Brenda. I laid some traps for him and he fell into them. He tried to knock me out in Central Park and to run me down in front of Helen Manning's. He was the only human being who knew I'd be there. Once I had cleared Helen of any complicity, it had to be Tom."

Ferguson went out to answer the telephone and came back to call David. When the latter returned he said, satisfaction in his face, "Keith isn't talking, but the facts do. They've found his tire marks in the mud outside Mary's house. Fedder's couple say that Tom was the only person they ever told about their daughter. He was such a sympathetic man. Winnie thinks he was there the evening Brenda was doped; she says he had been there a lot of times. They've found his fingerprints on the chaise longue where Julie was killed. He evidently didn't know that material can take prints. Little things, but they add up. Though, when you come down to it, it's your evidence that he killed Bill that will count. That's the murder they'll get him on."

Vic made no answer. When David had left him he settled down on a couch in the long drawing room where he lay thinking of the Benton twins at ten, at twelve, at fourteen; of the Benton twins at twenty-four, their short lives ended. Then at last he let himself remember Brenda's diary.

For the first few months of the year it had consisted of brief notations, appointments with hairdressers, for lunch, dinner, theaters, parties. After she took the job with Chuck Fedder there were fuller entries, as though she wanted to keep a record of this mad and amusing time. There were frequent references to Mary's separation from Tom.

With the breaking of the Ralston scandal she had become disturbed. She could not continue with the Fedders unless she was sure they were not involved. There was a brief comment: "Talked to Julie today. She swore they were not responsible for the contract but that the Markham angle was deliberate. Tom Keith was doing it."

Later she had scrawled, "Met Tom for lunch."

After that the tone of the diary changed.

"I didn't know love was like this. I'm happy. Happy!"

There were a number of pages blank except for the

words, "Committee hearing." Then there was an entry: "The hearings came to an end today. It's over at last, but nothing can ever again be the same. I feel unclean..."

"Yesterday I met a girl at the Cornings', Helen Manning, a beautiful creature. She's looking for a place to stay temporarily and I told her she could have Bill's room until he comes back. She thought I was being kind, but I need someone here so it won't be easy for Tom to come any more. I haven't the courage to refuse otherwise..."

"What have I done? I saw John Markham today and I was horrified. He looks so old and defeated..."

"Helen told me she was working for the government. She begged me to tell the truth, not just to clear John, but to undo the harm to the administration. She said a shadow of suspicion shakes people's confidence in their government. So I've got to do it. But I must tell Tom first..."

"Last night Julie sent me some sleeping pills. I took one. Just one. Tom dropped in because Helen had a date for the evening. Later I fell asleep. They had given me a lot of pills, Tom and Julie. They want me to die..."

*"Bound to thy service with unceasing care.* I loved you and you want me to be dead. To be so madly, so abjectly in love. I'm ashamed. And I can't help it. I can't help it! But I'm frightened. I've written Bill to come back. I'm going to take this diary up to the usual place. Some day it may help me to understand this madness."

Vic tried to shut away the thought of Brenda. As Mary came into the room with Helen he got up. The actress's make-up had been so skillfully applied that only her haunted eyes, the weary tremor of her lips betrayed her feelings. She held out her hands and stood on tiptoe to kiss him on both cheeks.

"Mary, forgive me if you can."

"I should ask you that, Vic. You saved my life

last night. Tom meant to take me with him, to shoot us both. He told me so while we waited in that dark little room. It didn't seem to matter then, with everything fallen to pieces, with all the good I knew in him destroyed. But today I know he had to be stopped, that this way is best. And some good has come of all the horror. John has been cleared."

"Are you up to the trip back to New York yet?" he asked, noticing that she wore a topcoat.

"I have a performance to give tonight," she reminded him.

"You're going to act tonight!" Helen said, startled.

"Why, of course. It's my job, you know." She flashed her famous smile and was gone with a wave of her hand.

"And tonight," Helen said in a tone of wonder, "she'll be making hundreds of people rock with laughter."

"Which is going to save her in the next few months," Vic said somberly.

"You mean the trial and the publicity?"

"All that, of course, plus the fact that there is no happy ending. I think she and Markham love each other and don't know it. Some day they'll find out, but they'll never be able to marry. There are always people who will say, 'Where there's smoke . . .' And the whole business will be raked up again. I hope to God Tom never realizes that. He would think it almost worthwhile if he could know he has spoiled their lives."

He drew her down on the big couch beside him. "I've spent the last few months worrying about other people's lives. Now I want to concentrate on my own —and yours. Will you marry me, Helen?"

She was laughing. "If you could see yourself! People would think I had to beat you into submission!"

He grinned at her. "The bruises will heal and the scars will fade. Will you have me, sweetheart? I love you so much." His hands tightened on hers. "Do you still think it's impossible for you to be in love with me?"

"Oh, that!" She leaned toward him, kissed his cheek. "That happened ages ago when I saw you in a concert. All this time I've been so—so jealous of Mary, thinking . . ." The rest of the words were blotted out against his mouth.

At length he said, "I'll start therapy at once. I called the doctor yesterday and he said there are some new techniques. I should be practicing in a few months. It will be dull for you, after the exciting job you've had. What are you going to do with yourself while I'm away on concert tours?"

"I'm not going to let you out of my sight," Helen said.

"Now that raises a problem." There was a glint of laughter, of something else, in his eyes. "It takes three days to get married in New York. What do you suggest?"

"I suggest," Helen said, "that we start back."

# How many of these Dell bestsellers have you read?

## DELL Bestseller List

1. **MILE HIGH** by Richard Condon $1.25
2. **THE AMERICAN HERITAGE DICTIONARY** 75c
3. **THE ANDROMEDA STRAIN** by Michael Crichton $1.25
4. **CATCH-22** by Joseph Heller 95c
5. **SOUL ON ICE** by Eldridge Cleaver 95c
6. **THE DOCTOR'S QUICK WEIGHT LOSS DIET** by Irwin M. Stillman, M.D., and Samm Sinclair Baker 95c
7. **THE DOCTOR'S QUICK INCHES-OFF DIET** by Irwin M. Stillman, M.D., and Samm Sinclair Baker 95c
8. **THE MIDAS COMPULSION** by Ivan Shaffer $1.25
9. **THE RICHEST MAN IN THE WORLD** by JP $1.25
10. **NEVER CRY WOLF** by Farley Mowat 50c

If you cannot obtain copies of these titles from your local bookseller, just send the price (plus 15c per copy for handling and postage) to Dell Books, Post Office Box 1000, Pinebrook, N.J. 07058. No postage or handling charge is required on any order of five or more books.

*Biggest dictionary value
ever offered in paperback!*

---

The Dell paperback edition of
# THE AMERICAN HERITAGE DICTIONARY
## OF THE ENGLISH LANGUAGE

- Largest number of entries—55,000
- 832 pages—nearly 300 illustrations
- The only paperback dictionary with photographs

---

These special features make this new, modern dictionary clearly superior to any comparable paperback dictionary:

- More entries and more illustrations than any other paperback dictionary
- The first paperback dictionary with photographs
- Words defined in modern-day language that is clear and precise
- Over one hundred notes on usage with more factual information than any comparable paperback dictionary
- Unique appendix of Indo-European roots
- Authoritative definitions of new words from science and technology
- More than one hundred illustrative quotations from Shakespeare to Salinger, Spenser to Sontag
- Hundreds of geographic and biographical entries
- Pictures of all the Presidents of the United States
- Locator maps for all the countries of the world

### A DELL BOOK 75c

If you cannot obtain copies of these titles from your local bookseller, just send the price (plus 15c per copy for handling and postage) to Dell Books, Post Office Box 1000, Pinebrook, N. J. 07058. No postage or handling charge is required on any order of five or more books.

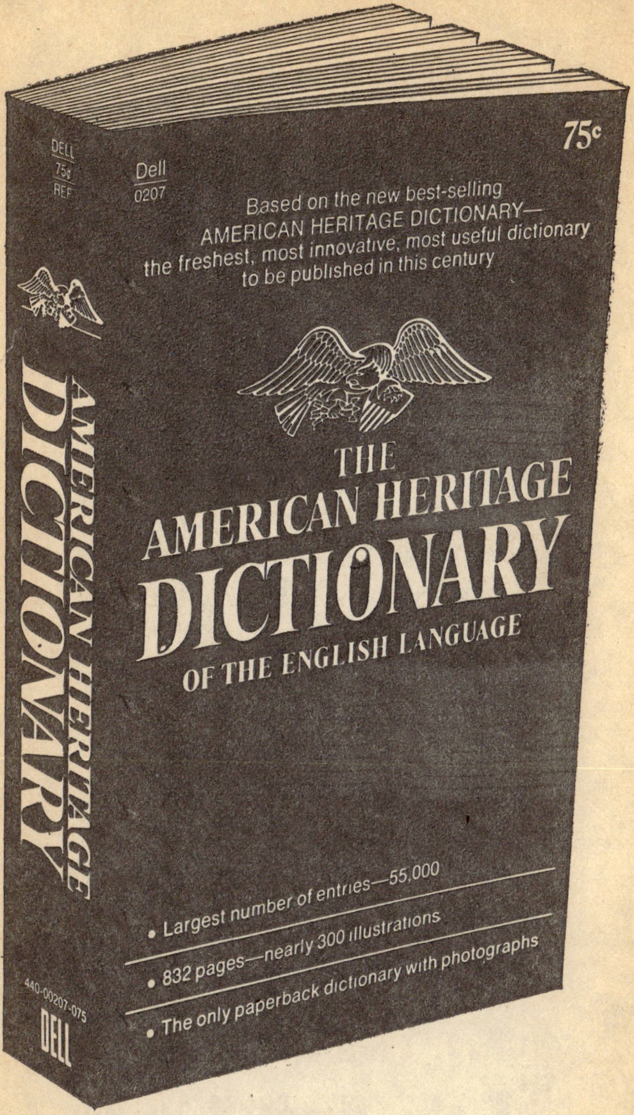

75¢
Dell
0207
Based on the new best-selling
AMERICAN HERITAGE DICTIONARY—
the freshest, most innovative, most useful dictionary
to be published in this century
THE
AMERICAN HERITAGE
DICTIONARY
OF THE ENGLISH LANGUAGE
• Largest number of entries—55,000
• 832 pages—nearly 300 illustrations
• The only paperback dictionary with photographs
DELL
75¢
REF
AMERICAN HERITAGE
DICTIONARY
440-00207-075
DELL

*Novels of Romance and Chilling Suspense . . .*

# GOTHIC MYSTERIES

by

Mary Roberts Rinehart

THE AFTER HOUSE 75c
ALIBI FOR ISABEL 75c
THE BAT 75c
THE BREAKING POINT 75c
THE CASE OF JENNIE BRYCE 75c
THE CIRCULAR STAIRCASE 75c
DANGEROUS DAYS 75c
THE DOCTOR 75c
THE DOOR 75c
THE GREAT MISTAKE 75c
LOST ECSTASY 75c
THE MAN IN LOWER TEN 75c
MARRIED PEOPLE 75c
MISS PINKERTON 75c
THE STRANGE ADVENTURE 75c
THE STREET OF SEVEN STARS 75c
THE SWIMMING POOL 75c
THE WALL 75c

DELL BOOKS

If you cannot obtain copies of these titles from your local bookseller, just send the price (plus 15c per copy for handling and postage) to Dell Books, Post Office Box 1000, Pinebrook, N. J. 07058. No postage or handling charge is required on any order of five or more books.